I0666998

Changeling Press LLC

ChangelingPress.com

Arcane Betrayal (Arcane Talents 6)
An Arcane Talents Christmas Romance
Angela Knight

Arcane Betrayal (Arcane Talents 6)
An Arcane Talents Christmas Romance
Angela Knight

All rights reserved.
Copyright ©2024 Angela Knight

ISBN: 978-1-60521-931-8

Publisher:
Changeling Press LLC
315 N. Centre St.
Martinsburg, WV 25404
ChangelingPress.com

Printed in the U.S.A.

Editor: Jean Cooper
Cover Artist: Angela Knight

The individual stories in this anthology have been previously released in E-Book format.

Table of Contents

Arcane Betrayal (Arcane Talents 6)
An Arcane Talents Christmas Romance
Angela Knight

Targeted by terrorists, a woman inhabited by a tiger spirit turns to the lover she left behind.

Margay Whitfield has a mystical bond to a tiger spirit which allows her to call on the animal's power -- until a terrorist bombing leaves her with PTSD and shaky control over her inner big cat. Now she's come home to Ashburg, S.C., where her mother owns a restaurant. Margay hopes that a simple, boring job will give her the time and peace to heal her psychic wounds and rebuild her control over Razia, her tiger. But when the terrorists who attacked her in Ukraine use Raz to turn the town against her and her mother, she has to call a cop.

Though Ashburg Police Chief Grant Sawyer has no magical abilities at all, he and Margay were childhood best friends -- and high school sweethearts. But ten years of tragedy has left Margay with deep psychological wounds and a fear she could hurt -- even kill -- the man she loves. Can Margay and Grant defeat the terrorists despite the odds, and rediscover their lost love?

Chapter One

"It's all right," the voice said, low and soothing, though its owner smelled of fear. "You're fine. You're home. Nobody's going to hurt you. Wake up now, honey… Come on, you're scaring your mama."

Disoriented, Margay Whitfield blinked. For a moment, she had no idea where she was. At last, misfiring synapses got it together, and she realized she was standing in the apartment's living room.

Home. I'm home. Relief blasted through her, so sharp and fierce her knees almost buckled. *Home.* Home in Ashburg, SC. Not on the Charivnyk military base, where her whole damn life had exploded, leaving her career and sanity in flaming ruins.

It had only been a dream.

Her mother stood planted in her path, evidently trying to stop Margay from doing… whatever she'd been about to do while her sleepwalking mind was out to lunch.

"I know it was a bad one," Jocelyn Whitfield said, her voice with its soft southern accent low and soothing. "But all that's over now. You're home and safe." Comfortably plump, she was several inches shorter than Margay. Though fifty-six, Mama was still lovely, with round, prominent cheekbones, big dark eyes, a regal nose, and a generous mouth that usually stretched in a smile, despite its current tight, anxious line. Her yellow silk bathrobe seemed to glow against her dark skin, a match for the silk scarf wrapped protectively around her thick box braids. She was illuminated by the kind of soft golden glow Margay associated with magic. And that meant…

Oh, hell, I'm manifested. Sure enough, Margay

realized she was peering at her mother through the glowing feline mask of her cat spirit. Her body was cocooned in the tiger-shaped magical shell she and her Familiar had conjured in her sleep. Razia rumbled, the sound reverberating in her bones. The spirit's anxiety made Margay want to jump out of her skin. *No wonder Mama's looking paranoid.*

"She's not growling at you, Mama," Margay said, willing Razia's magic to disperse. Raz fought her, the manifestation's long striped tail whipping back and forth so hard, it hit the coffee table and sent it skidding across the hardwood floor. Something -- presumably the nightmare they'd had -- had the tiger seriously stirred up.

Which could be bad. Margay sniffed but didn't scent any blood with her cat's keen senses. Nor did Jocelyn seem to be bleeding. "Did I hurt you?"

Her mother relaxed, apparently reassured Margay was finally tracking. "No, honey, you just had a nightmare. Everything's fine. Why don't you go back to bed? It's only four in the morning."

She felt her muscles pull tight. "What did I do?"

Even the fake smile fled. "You were screaming about the bomb."

"Oh. That one." There were other nightmares -- the girls' school, the Marine convoy attack -- but it was the bomb that most upset Raz. Which probably stood to reason, given that was how the tiger died. "Sorry I woke you." *Again.*

Her mother smiled, and this time it looked more genuine. "Don't worry about it, honey. You know me, I can always nap. But you really need more rest. You don't sleep enough, and it's not good for you."

And risk that *dream again? Hell, no.* "I've got to burn some of this adrenaline off -- Raz is really wired."

Mama frowned. "You can't go running like that, honey. Somebody'll see you."

And the last thing they needed was to get Ashburg's Humanists stirred up. Margay concentrated, and this time Razia acquiesced with a feline grumble. The tiger manifestation disappeared, leaving the room illuminated only by Christmas lights from the seven-foot artificial tree standing beside one of the apartment's arched windows, decorated with the Hallmark ornaments Mama had collected for years.

The living area still smelled of cinnamon, apple, and nutmeg from the fresh batch of Christmas cookies her mother had baked that evening. And faintly, Mama's alchemical magic.

That scent alone was enough to make Margay's jangled nerves settle. Razia's restless rumble subsided.

Jocelyn studied her, frowning in concern. "You sure you don't want me to brew you something?"

It was a tempting thought. Her mother's alchemical Talent might not be strong enough for a pharmaceutical job, but any tea she brewed would put Margay right to sleep. But... "Honestly, I'll probably have another nightmare if I don't run some of this off. But you've got a lot of hungry people to feed -- you should try to get another couple of hours at least."

"All right." But Mama still didn't look happy. "Be careful out there. It always makes me nervous when you go running at night."

"I'm bulletproof, remember? Besides, Ashburg isn't exactly Falluja." Or Charivnyk, for that matter, not that she could ever breathe a word about that.

Judging from the look her mother shot her, Jocelyn wasn't reassured. "Fine, but if you run into Jimmy Miller again, keep your temper. We don't need that kind of trouble."

* * *

Dressed in thick black leggings, a gold U.S. Arcane Corps Academy sweatshirt, socks and running shoes, Margay headed down the steep, narrow stairs to the street. They'd lived over Mama's Spoon -- the restaurant her grandmother had founded in the 70s -- since she'd been a kid. When she opened the door that led to the street, she found the December night clear and cold beyond it.

Combat-trained habit had her scanning her surroundings. The sun wasn't up yet, but the street was lit by ornate black streetlamps wreathed in Christmas lights.

The restaurant's plate-glass window stretched off to her right, the words "Mama's Spoon" painted in an elaborate script over a cartoon of a serving spoon steaming magical sparks.

Across the street, Ashburg's town park lay still under a starry night sky, its oaks, pines and maples dark silhouettes around the shapes of playground equipment. In the center of it all loomed a towering cedar, swathed in Christmas lights blinking on and off in slow, hypnotic patterns.

Farther down, brick storefronts lined either side of Main Street, the buildings shoulder to shoulder, each one as familiar to Margay as an elderly aunt. Plate-glass windows displayed manger scenes, Santas, or mannequins in their holiday best, trying to pull in procrastinating shoppers in these last few days before Christmas.

The Ashburg Savings and Loan loomed next to the Standard, a department store that dated back to the Fifties. Next came the clothing consignment store, A Second Chance at Style, followed by Shear Elegance, the beauty salon her mother frequented. Across from them stood a furniture store, an office supply, a pizza joint called Billy's, and Six Shooters, a bar. There was even a comic book shop named Tangled Web that Margay and Grant Sawyer had spent most of their teen years haunting.

The Great Recession had closed many of the other businesses Margay remembered from her childhood, but Ashburg was undergoing something of a renaissance. None of the shops were boarded up now, and there was even a Food Lion and a Burger King at the end of the main drag.

No people, though. Ashburg's version of the morning rush wouldn't start for several hours yet. She had the dregs of the night to herself.

Margay turned to brace both hands against the Spoon's brick wall and leaned in, stretching out her hamstrings.

Razia rumbled, making the air vibrate around them.

The tiger had been far more skittish than usual lately. During the wars, Margay would have started looking for snipers. The cat's ability to sense incoming bullet storms had always been considerably better than hers.

The trouble was, the cat spirit communicated in images and emotion, and sometimes it was hard to determine exactly what she was worked up about. *We aren't at war anymore*, Margay told her. *Nobody's trying to kill us.*

Raz growled, apparently disagreeing.

As if on cue, she felt the world drift sideways under her feet -- and she was back in Charivnyk.

It glowed on the concrete floor just beyond the bars, reeking of petrochemicals and the ozone stink of magic. In the cage next to Razia's, Czar roared, the sound wild with helpless terror and frustrated rage...

This isn't real, Margay told herself fiercely, though she could *see* the bomb right in front of her. Not a memory -- a razor-blade-sharp hallucination. She squeezed her eyes shut as every muscle in her neck jerked tight. Leaning hard into the Spoon's wall, she used the sensation of rough brick under her hands to ground herself in the present and fight off the flashback.

She started sucking cold air in through her nose for a count of four, held it for another four-count and blew it out for four more, trying to short-circuit the lethal memory before it could trigger another manifestation. The stink of RDX explosives began to thin as she breathed. *It's not real, I'm at home, I'm safe...*

The nightmare vision finally faded, leaving her sagging against the wall in the cold December night.

Okay. Better. Margay straightened away from the bricks and headed down the sidewalk, forcing herself not to break into a full-out run. This shit wasn't something she could outrun.

Her breath pluming white around her, she lengthened her strides into a lope, then a jog. Not running from anything. Definitely not.

Deep in her mind, Raz crouched, just the tip of her tail flicking, ears pricked as she scanned the street with every sense, magical and otherwise. It had been only six months since the tiger died, and the trauma had left her hyper-vigilant.

It hadn't done great things for Margay either.

She turned down a side street and began to pick up the pace. The moon was a bare sliver peeking through the clouds, silvering the roofs of the houses lining the road. Christmas lights festooned rooftops and porches, and inflated Santas and snowmen lit yards. With Raz providing feline night vision, it might as well be daylight.

Margay had no trouble spotting the hulking silhouette of a police SUV. It sat parked in the entrance to a side street just ahead.

Oh hell, it's Jimmy Fucking Miller. Ready to pull out and chase my ass.

It took all her willpower to keep Razia's growl from vibrating the air around them. What the hell was the cop doing on this side of town at this time of night?

When she'd realized Jimmy was a Humanist, Margay had made it her business to learn his patrol route. He should be at the other end of his zone now.

I do not *need this shit. Not tonight. Maybe I should turn around and run the other way…*

Her Familiar growled and sent her a particularly bloody mental image. Margay grimaced. *No, Raz, we are* not *going to eat him. Besides, he's such an asshole, he'd probably taste like a dirty diaper.*

But maybe he hadn't spotted her. Could be slacking again. She'd caught Miller sleeping in his vehicle before.

Margay lengthened her stride, hoping to streak by so fast, he wouldn't notice her. She'd been a high school track star even before she'd gotten Raz. Now there wasn't a norm alive who could catch her when she hit her afterburners.

She flew past the SUV…

And the Ford Interceptor's headlights flicked on.

Fuck. Try to lose the bastard? No, she wouldn't put it past him to shoot her and claim he'd thought she was fleeing the scene of a crime.

The SUV turned after her as she pounded along, its headlights lighting up the road ahead of her.

Not to mention my back. Her shoulder blades began to itch, and Raz tried to manifest. Margay clamped down, wrestling her Familiar for control. Miller wouldn't be able to shoot her through her manifestation -- not with a handgun, anyway -- but in Raz's current mood, she might kill him.

I'm just gonna have to deal with him and hope he's not bored enough to invent a reason to arrest me. Swear to God, if he tries anything else, I'm reporting him to Grant. If it hadn't felt so much like tattling, she'd have done it already.

Margay slowed to a walk and threw up both hands to show she was unarmed, then turned, pasting a pleasant smile on her face. She started back toward the SUV, her dark-adapted eyes stinging in the blinding glare of its headlights. Sweat trickled down her spine as her shoulder muscles knotted. She badly wanted to manifest, but if Raz got control…

As she reached the SUV's driver's side, the vehicle rolled to a stop, the window humming down. The vehicle's dashboard lights lit a familiar handsome, angular face. "Hey, it's me." The voice was a deep, slow southern drawl that was blessedly familiar -- and did *not* belong to Jimmy Miller. "And yeah, I can see you're not armed."

Grant Sawyer, Ashburg Police Chief.

The tension ran out of Margay so fast, her knees almost buckled. In her mind, Razia sank back down on her belly, chainsaw growl dying. "I thought this was Miller's shift."

"Jimmy's grandmother died." His tone sounded a little dry. "I'm covering his zone for him." Given the department consisted of only seven sworn officers, even the chief sometimes worked a patrol shift.

"Jimmy's hard on grandmothers," Margay

observed, just as dry. "That's what, the fourth granny he's had kick it?"

"He claims it's his step-grandmother."

"You do realize Jimmy's a lying sack of shit?"

"Yeah, but his uncle's the mayor." Grant looked her over and his smile bled into a frown. "You look like hell. What's wrong?"

"I've been having trouble sleeping."

"How's Raz? I thought I heard a roar twenty minutes ago."

Margay winced. If he'd heard it, so had half the town. Just what she and Mom did *not* need. "Had a nightmare."

He eyed her, his gaze perceptive, concerned. "Want to get in and talk about it?"

For a moment, she was seriously tempted, but that would be asking for trouble. "That… probably isn't a good idea for either of us. You never know who's watching in this town. And if they're watching, they're talking."

"Let 'em talk -- neither of us is married. But if it makes you feel better…" He threw the SUV into park, shut off the engine, and got out.

Though he was only a couple of inches taller than she was, Grant had a powerful, athletic build that his Ashburg police uniform showed off to advantage. His dark hair curled despite its short cut, sweeping back from a widow's peak that called attention to the intensely masculine lines of his face with its broad, square jaw and cleft chin. But his mouth looked soft.

Was soft. Looking at those lips made Margay remember how they'd tasted.

And judging by the way his gaze heated as he looked at her, his memories were just as tempting. "I've been wanting to talk to you since you got home."

But I don't want to talk to you. It's not safe for either of us. But saying as much would hurt him, and Margay couldn't do that to the man who'd been her bestie since third grade. "Shouldn't you be out on patrol?" She grimaced. "Unless you think I've been burglarizing Main Street."

Grant frowned, dark brows snapping down over narrowing eyes that would be green in better light. "That sounds oddly specific." He paused, visibly putting two and two together. "Has Miller been giving you shit?"

Yes. "No," she lied with a sunny smile. "The mayor's Humanist nephew would never give me a hard time."

A muscle flexed in Grant's jaw. "Damn it, I warned that son of a bitch…"

Margay sighed. "You're not going to be able to work your way up to a bigger department if the mayor fires you for canning the family asshole." Grant had wanted to be a cop as long as she'd wanted to be a member of the Arcane Corps.

"I don't give a damn! He's abusing his authority. I hate cops like that. It's hard to argue 'All Cops *Aren't* Bastards' when you keep giving badges to actual bastards."

Grant always had wanted to fix things. He'd never seemed to realize that sometimes things didn't *want* to be fixed. And they were prone to blow you to hell if you tried.

He eyed her a bit suspiciously. "Just what has Miller been doing to you?"

Crap, he'd fire Miller and make an enemy out of the mayor if she didn't nip this in the bud. "Do you seriously think some norm bigot could be a threat to *me*?"

"Given that he's three inches taller, outweighs you by forty pounds *and* has a badge? Yeah, I do."

"Grant, I can manifest a three-hundred-pound tiger."

"But you won't," Grant said. "Because that would make trouble for your mom, and you'd rather put up with an abusive prick than do that." He studied her, then said slowly, "But Jimmy's not the real problem. What's going on, Margay? Why do I keep hearing Raz roar in the middle of the night?"

"She *died*, Grant. That tends to make a girl pissy."

"Yeah, but how? Your cat shouldn't even have been in the line of fire. We aren't at war anymore. Was it a training accident or what?"

"I could tell you, but I'd have to kill you. And then I'd have to do all that paperwork."

He frowned, ignoring the feeble joke. "Was it Ukraine?"

He'd always been sharp. "The United States government does not have boots on the ground in Ukraine."

"That's Uncle Sam -- never where he shouldn't be. Is that why you've been avoiding me?"

"I haven't been avoiding you." She'd been avoiding the hell out of him.

"I still…" His lips shaped a word beginning with L, but he changed it at the last minute. "…Care about you."

"Is that why your marriage imploded?" The minute the words were out of her mouth, Margay winced. "Hell, Grant, I didn't mean that."

"My marriage imploded because my wife cheated on me." There was so little emotion in his voice, Margay knew it had to have hurt. She also knew Brandy McAllister insisted to all and sundry that she'd only cheated because Grant was still in love with Margay. Which was bullshit -- they hadn't been together since high school.

Still, Margay owed him the truth. Or at least as much of it as she could legally tell. "I've been avoiding you because Raz isn't stable. She isn't -- *we* aren't -- safe. The Corps psychologist tells me it will be at least another six months. Maybe longer than that because... It wasn't a good death." *Light exploded inside her in a stunning blast of agony as Razia roared in terror. Savage heat and pressure built within her, stinking of RDX...* "It's left us a little... raw. She's easy to set off, and that could be bad."

He studied her in the illumination of the SUV's headlights. "I talked to Jake Nolan, a Feral cop I know who was in the Corps. He said there are assets that you can use. The VA..."

"Yeah, Veterans Affairs got me my therapist." Hearing the snap in her own voice, she drew in a deep breath. "Look, Mama's teas have helped, and I have a prescription for when things get bad. We'll get through this. But trying to have a relationship... It would be too much for me right now. Not with Raz still adjusting. It will get better" -- *or at least I fucking hope so* --"but I've got to get through the next six months without doing anything unforgivable."

His broad shoulders slumped. "Yeah, I understand you've got a lot going on right now. You don't need to juggle a love affair on top of it." He reached out and took her hand. His hand felt strong and warm. "But I'm still your friend. And I'll always be here for you."

* * *

Grant Sawyer stared down into Margay's lovely

oval face. As always, those big, Feral gold eyes fascinated him. They seemed to glow against the warm brown of her skin in the illumination from the SUV's dash lights.

She wore no lipstick on her wide, full mouth, and her white teeth flashed as she spoke. Her long black hair was woven into countless thin braids, with other strands left curling loose. He'd Googled it, and the style was called goddess braids. Which, as far as he was concerned, was an entirely appropriate 'do for Margay Whitfield. All that hair was tied in a swinging tail that hung to her pert, perfect ass.

Since she wore only leggings and a United States Arcane Corps sweatshirt, he could tell she was as fit as she'd been in high school. Curves everywhere curves should be, and lean muscle everywhere else.

God, he wanted her. Her wide nostrils flared, and he had the uncomfortable feeling she could see the hunger in his eyes, smell it in his scent.

She was even more beautiful than back when he'd dreamed of a future with her. Before the Arcane Corps -- and something seriously nasty -- had put that look in her Feral gold eyes.

Grant had been sitting in his vehicle working on a report when some instinct made him glance up to see a dark figure darting by. Running so fast his jaw dropped.

Then she'd shot in front of his headlights, and he'd recognized Margay. Her braids flew behind her as she ran, long legs flashing as her arms pumped. She'd been running full out, nothing held back, and her face gleamed with sweat even in the cold. She'd worn an expression of such desperation and pain, his heart clenched in his chest.

So he'd started his vehicle and pulled out after

her. When she'd turned back to him, he'd instantly read the fear behind her wide, tight smile.

He couldn't stand the thought of scaring Margay Whitfield. Yet even after he'd identified himself -- even after he'd gotten out of the SUV -- the unease remained.

Why the hell would she look at *him* like that? Why had she been ducking him? They'd grown up best friends -- caught frogs as nine-year-olds, watched anime in middle school, geeked out together about SF novels, comics and films as teens. Gone to Dragon Con in Atlanta every year, collecting selfies and cosplaying as superheroes or anime or gaming characters. Shared their first kiss. Gone to prom. Made love.

Loved.

And yeah, Brandy had been right -- Grant had loved Margay more than he'd ever loved his wife.

He'd understood why Margay had walked away from him after high school. She'd wanted to join the Arcane Corps ever since they'd been kids. After all, her father had been a Corps vet with a magical tiger of his own. So Grant hadn't resented it -- much -- when she'd left to join the Corps. He'd wanted to be a cop just as bad.

She'd succeeded in her goal, just as he had, only to leave the Corps and come home. And the rumor was she had the kind of wounds that didn't show.

Grant had tried more than once to talk to her -- even showing up at her mother's restaurant -- but she'd just shaken her head and said she was busy.

He knew her injuries weren't physical -- that long, smooth body was whole. She still moved with the same fluid strength and confidence. Jocelyn had told him she'd come back injured to the soul. But there were scars in those golden eyes.

Before Grant could think of a way to reach her now, the radio handset on his shoulder gave a demanding crackle. "Ashburg I-1, you've got a 10-80 at 156 Jones St."

He cursed silently and triggered the handset clipped to his shoulder as he turned back to his SUV. "Ashburg I-1, en route." He released the transmit button and told her, "I've got to take this."

Margay frowned, worry in her eyes, and half started after him. "What's a 10-80?"

"Domestic violence call." He curled his lip in disgust. "Sounds like Sam Jenkins beat the hell out of his girlfriend again."

"You need backup? I could go with you."

Because of course she would. Everything else might be gone to shit, but Margay would always have his back. "Thanks, but I've got it."

She frowned, visibly worrying. "But what if this asshole has a gun? I'm bulletproof and you're not."

"And if you were a cop, I'd love to have you. But you're not, and if something happened, the liability would eat the town alive."

At that, she deflated. "Yeah, it wouldn't be a good idea to put Raz in that situation anyway. It'd be too likely to set her off." With a sigh, Margay waved him on. "Better go answer your call."

She watched as he slid into his vehicle. When he glanced into his rearview mirror as he drove away, she was still staring after him.

As if, despite her cat, despite whatever the hell had happened to her, she still cared.

Christ knew he did.

* * *

Hours later, Margay stood in the Mama's Spoon

dish pit with her hands plunged into hot soapy water, using a stiff brush to scrub burned-on macaroni off a baking pan to get it ready for the Hobart industrial dishwasher.

She'd hated this job when she was a kid. Spent hours elbow-deep in soapy water, daydreaming of being in the Corps. Of bonding with a big cat like Daddy's, going to exotic places and fighting bad guys to defend democracy.

Now here she was, right back in hot, soapy water. Ironically, she found she no longer minded the job. It was stress-free -- or least, nobody was shooting at her. That was enough for now.

Margay looked around at the kitchen, feeling her neck muscles relax. The Spoon was just as much home as the apartment upstairs, though Jocelyn had done some major renovations since Margay's childhood.

The kitchen had been redesigned for maximum efficiency and traffic flow. There were two gas ovens, a griddle, a pair of fryers, and assorted other gear, most of it purchased with the money Jocelyn had won on *Magical Kitchens* three years before.

Doors led to a pair of walk-ins -- a huge chiller for refrigerated foods and an even larger freezer for frozen items. Shelving held dry ingredients, dishes or pots and pans, along with stainless steel tables organized for different kinds of meal preparation. The walls were covered with black and white tile for easy cleanup. Arcane spell circles were painted on the black concrete floor in front of prep stations, allowing Jocelyn and her two alchemist assistants to use magic to turn every dish into something special.

Margay wasn't an alchemist, but she could feel the smooth flow of magic through the big room. The air was redolent with the smell of cooking food, herbs, and spices. The combination had meant home and safety for so long, just being here felt like a benediction.

God, she *needed* this. It was why she'd come back, though the idea of running home to Mama was humiliating for a grown-ass woman. The fact was, working at the Spoon was her best hope of regaining her shaky mental health.

Besides, there was something so simple and satisfying about scrubbing something clean. Nobody's life hung in the balance, and baked-on macaroni was no match for a melded Feral's strength.

Unfortunately, her mind kept drifting back to this morning's encounter with Grant. Though she'd run into him a few times since she'd returned, it had been years since they'd spoken at any length. He'd gone to work for the Laurel County Sheriff's Office the next county over, and they'd rarely crossed paths in the decade since.

The contrast between the cute high school boy she'd loved and the handsome, capable police chief couldn't have been sharper.

Still, Margay had texted him to make sure he was okay after she'd gotten home. She'd known the worry was ridiculous -- he'd been a cop for a decade. Grant could take care of himself, normie or not.

He'd texted back to say he was busy booking Sam Jenkins in at the county jail on aggravated domestic violence charges. The bastard had fought, but Grant had dragged his ass in anyway.

Wish I could have seen that. Big, broad-shouldered Grant, kicking ass and taking names -- Batman with a badge.

Raz rumbled softly in her mind, a thrumming sound that was the tiger version of a purr. The cat had hated the fuck out of Margay's ex, Austin Reynolds, but she thoroughly approved of Grant.

Too bad I'm so fucked up he's better off without me.

Chapter Two

Austin Reynolds and the Russian stood on the sidewalk in front of the Spoon, waiting for their cue.

Despite the December chill, the sun beat down on Austin's head, made worse by the full-body Spook Suit that magically bent light around him. The sensation of being slowly suffocated was exacerbated by the suit's Spider-Man-like mask, which covered his head completely, including goggles over his eyes. He longed to take the mask off, but a floating, disembodied head would attract a little too much attention.

Then there was his Familiar's seething growl, which vibrated the air around him. Given they were hanging out on Ashburg's Main Street at fucking noon, the racket wasn't exactly good for their cover. Despite Austin's invisibility, anybody who heard the sound would wonder where the hell it was coming from.

What's more, the constant rumble was getting on Austin's last nerve. Worse, it was getting on *Karl*'s nerves, and Austin suspected that wasn't good for his continued health.

Rodin Karl Makarovich might be nothing more than an Arcanist, but he was one of the scariest motherfuckers Austin had ever met. Given Austin could manifest a magical six-hundred-pound Amur tiger, his standard for scary motherfucker was high.

"You're growling again," Karl's deep male voice said in his earbud on their encrypted comms system. "Shut cat the fuck up." Irritation made his Russian accent even thicker than normal, though when he chose, he could sound as American as any Southern good ol' boy.

Get over it, Czar, Austin thought viciously, grinding his will against that of the cat spirit who shared his body. *I did what I did, and there's nothing you can do about it. If I die, you die too. We've already established you don't want to die.*

Otherwise, the spirit wouldn't have rushed into Austin's body when the explosion killed Czar.

The tiger fell silent, though he made sure Austin couldn't ignore his mental image: crouched and staring, ears pinned. The question was, would the tiger decide to sound off at the worst possible moment -- and would Austin be able to silence him if he did?

Uneasy, Austin closed his eyes to look for the Russian, invisible in a Spook Suit of his own. Sure enough, Karl's magical aura lit up the darkness just feet away.

Normally no Arcanist could intimidate Austin -- he and Czar had a hell of a lot more power than any Arc ever born. But the GRU agent was a head taller than he was. And at a muscular 6'1", Austin was no pussy.

The big blond was also built like the Terminator and radiated more menace than Chernobyl. Austin strongly suspected the Russian knew fifty ways to kill him, Czar notwithstanding -- and was giving the selection serious thought.

Austin's hand curled into a fist as he eyed the agent's sullen magical glow. *I can still rip his fucking head off and there wouldn't be a damned thing he could do about it.*

But if Karl struck when he wasn't expecting it... That would be bad.

Czar chuffed, the sound contemptuous.

Shut the fuck up. Blow this and we're both dead! If the Russian doesn't get us, the Feds will.

And then there was the problem of Margay. Her cat might be only half the size of his, but if you pissed her off, she'd still make sure you had a really bad day.

Flag-draped casket bad.

Leaning a shoulder against the brick wall, Austin extended his head to peer through the Spoon's plate-glass window, scanning for her.

The restaurant looked like a typical southern diner. Red leather booths lined the room, framing sturdy oak tables. Poster-size photos hung on the walls, most of them shots from that television show Margay's mother had won three years before. An elaborately decorated Christmas tree towered in a corner, white lights blinking, red and gold ornaments nestled among its branches.

At the opposite end of the room, Margay pushed through the swinging door carrying a plastic bin. She strode toward a booth littered with the remains of someone's meal.

How far the mighty have fallen. Decorated Arcane Corps hero to bussing tables in the space of six months. *Serves the bitch right.*

Though if she happened to close her eyes and spot the glow of his Spook Suit… Austin pulled out of view, knowing if he blew their cover, Anastasia would be pissed.

Besides, he wanted this to go off as planned. After the way Margay had nuked their plans in Charivnyk, she deserved to be taught a lesson. Needed to learn she wasn't the hot shit war hero she -- and the Arcane Corps -- imagined her to be.

"On my way," Anastasia purred in his earbud, snapping him out of a pleasant fantasy of tearing out Margay's throat. As always, the silken sound of the Bard's voice hit him like a drug.

Turning, Austin watched his lover stroll along the sidewalk toward them, looking like any American woman on her way to lunch. Spies were supposed to be bland, nondescript people, but Uvarova Anastasia Yakovna had never gotten the memo. Instead of a Spook Suit, she wore a sweeping black wool trench that flared around her as she walked. Black trousers hugged her long legs, tucked into knee-high boots, and a red turtleneck called attention to the mouth-watering swell of her gorgeous breasts. Dark hair fell slick and smooth around her slim shoulders. She had the face of a Bond girl, angular yet delicate, with eyes of a brilliant, icy blue.

And she was taking a hell of a risk. What if Margay saw her? If the cunt remembered…

He dared another glance through the window. Margay was gone, leaving the table clean behind her.

"Tiger is growling again," Karl murmured in his earbud.

"Austin, darling, go wait across the street," Anastasia said, her lips barely moving as she spoke over the comms unit she wore in one ear. "We can't afford a misstep."

"Roger that." The heat of humiliated rage seared his cheekbones, but Austin knew she was right. He turned and stalked across the road to the town's tiny excuse for a park, dodging a car whose driver couldn't see him. *Damn it, Czar, why can't you keep your fucking mouth shut?*

Czar responded with a louder rumble. This time the tiger sounded amused.

Fuck you too, Cat.

He took up a post near the park's Christmas tree and turned in time to see Anastasia open the Spoon's door. She hesitated as if checking out the interior, a pause designed to let Karl slip past her with the MEED. Then she stepped inside.

Now, Margay, you little bitch, you'll finally get what you deserve. Adrenaline sizzled in Austin's blood. His mouth dust dry, he forced himself to breathe deeply and slowly to control his racing heartbeat.

"Package in position," Karl reported minutes later in that iced-vodka-over-gravel voice. "Preparing to leave restaurant."

But the door remained shut, since it opening on its own would attract attention. The norms couldn't see Karl's magic, but Margay could. If she realized someone in a Spook Suit was present, the whole op would go sideways. The Russian was going to have to wait for someone to leave.

Five minutes went by. Ten. If Austin had been manifested, his tail would be twitching.

Twenty minutes passed before the restaurant's door opened and a middle-aged man in paint-splattered clothes left the building. The door seemed to hesitate as it swung shut behind him -- Karl slipping out after him.

"Exited building," the Russian murmured, sounding as bored as if he were listing his morning's breakfast.

"Make the call," Anastasia breathed. "Don't forget to alter your voice."

I'm not an idiot, Austin thought, annoyed. "Roger that." Drawing on his magic, he prepared to use it to vibrate the air, just as Czar had been doing all damn day. He thought about generating a woman's voice, then decided to use a man's. Something a bit higher than his own, more like a tenor…

* * *

Jocelyn stood in the permanent spell circle painted on the kitchen floor at the main prep counter, humming to a chicken breast as she coated it in the blend of flour, spices and magical herbs she grew in pots upstairs.

Carefully, she concentrated on the satisfaction and enjoyment she wanted her customers to experience -- the crunch of the coating, the smoky flavor of the seasonings, the moist, juicy chicken. The energy of the Earth's magical field poured from the Arcane circle painted on the floor beneath her feet, flooding her body and making her fingers buzz with alchemical power.

Normally, Jocelyn found cooking soothing. There was nothing more satisfying than feeding people. Yet today, she found herself having to work at it harder than usual.

Raz was growling, a low, agitated rumble she didn't think her daughter was even aware of. Otherwise, Margay would do something to stop it. The tiger hadn't been this bad since her daughter had gotten home.

What the hell was going on with that cat? For that matter, what was going on with Margay, and why wouldn't she talk about it? Had to be some kind of government secret. There'd been things Darrell had refused to talk about either, even after he'd been out of the Arcane Corps for decades.

Whatever was bothering Margay was worse. Bad enough to have killed her tiger and left her with the kind of nightmares that woke her screaming.

Or in Raz's case, roaring.

Jocelyn flicked a glance over at her daughter as she scrubbed a nearby prep counter. Margay's neck and shoulders were visibly tight. Jocelyn closed her eyes and studied her through closed lids. A glowing tiger crouched in the darkness where Margay should be, tail lashing restlessly -- the embodiment of the Familiar spirit's magic.

The tips of her fingers grew hot, and she snapped her gaze to the breading bowl. *Damn it, get your mind back on the job before this bird ends up tasting like ass and grief.*

She eyed the chicken breast. *Can't risk it.* Grimacing in disgust, Jocelyn threw it into the trashcan beside the counter. The problem with being an alchemist was that your bad mood had a nasty way of affecting whatever you were cooking. Norm chefs could wallow in rage and drama without changing the taste of a dish one bit. She had to be a lot more disciplined.

"Hey, Jos!" Nancy called from the dining room. "Phone for you."

"Take a message!"

"He says he wants you to cater a wedding. Needs to talk to you now."

Her first impulse was to tell Nancy the guy could damn well call back after lunch. Unfortunately, catering made up too much of the Spoon's business, and people with money didn't give a damn about anybody else's schedule.

And *of course*, he'd called in on the landline instead of the Spoon's cell. She really needed to get rid of that dinosaur of a phone, but some older customers still called in on it. Grumbling under her breath, Jocelyn stepped to the sink to wash her hands, then stalked to the front of the house.

Her friend stood behind the counter where the old rotary phone stood beside the Square station that served as a register. As Jocelyn moved around the counter to take the big black handset from Nancy, her foot kicked something solid. Automatically, she glanced down, but there wasn't anything there. Frowning downward, she said, "Jocelyn Whitfield, Mama's Spoon. How may I help you?"

The bastard promptly hung up.

Irritated and way too tired on waaaay too little sleep, Jocelyn glared at the handset before slamming it back into its cradle.

A thunderous *bang*! went off at her feet, followed an instant later by a crackling, popping fusillade. As she leaped back, something burned its way across her right thigh. Jocelyn screamed in startled pain as Nancy grabbed her by the arm and hauled her away. More bangs sounded as burning paper flew everywhere and the air filled with smoke. Backpedaling, Jocelyn tripped and fell, dragging Nancy down with her.

Startled screams and curses rang from the lunch crowd around them, people either leaping to their feet, diving under booth tables, or freezing in panic.

"Fireworks!" Nancy shouted in Jocelyn's ear over the explosions. "It's just firecrackers!"

But it sounds just like gunfire…

Which was when it hit her. *Oh, sweet Lord Jesus -- Margay!*

* * *

One minute, Margay was loading a plastic tray of pots into the Hobart. The next, a rolling volley of gunfire went off, echoed heartbeat later by her mother's scream. *Mama!*

Raz roared, sweeping her up and cocooning her in a magical tiger manifestation. They whirled and charged through the kitchen past the crew, bursting through swinging doors into the dining room.

The air was full of blue smoke, the reek of nitrocellulose and panicked screams…

Pain and fire detonated inside her, the pressure searing as Raz roared. Every heartbeat they could contain the blast meant someone else wouldn't die. She could hear animals roaring, humans screaming, knew she had to save them, but the pressure built and built and built, and she knew she couldn't hold it, knew they were going to die…

Then she was back in the dining room, surrounded by customers, her mother wide-eyed with terror. But the air smelled wrong -- not like the Spoon at all. Reeking of smoke and ringing with screams. Margay froze, suddenly not sure where she was -- home, Ukraine, the Middle East… Where was she, *when* was she…

Time collapsed again. *The Familiars were roaring, pain filling Margay and Raz in a hot, expanding fireball about to blast them apart…*

* * *

Anastasia Yakovna lay on the floor beneath the booth's table, her cell phone pointed at the tiger manifestation crouching a few feet away. The cat bared its teeth at Jocelyn Whitfield, a savage snarl vibrating the air. *Oh, this is perfect! She doesn't know her own mother!*

The hallucinogenic potion packaged with the fireworks was having its intended effect, triggering Whitfield's greatest vulnerability: her PTSD. That GRU Alchemist was damned impressive -- successfully targeting one specific person with that drug couldn't have been easy. In minutes, this restaurant could well be an abattoir. It all depended on how much control the woman had over her cat. *Hopefully, very little.*

Anastasia intended to video the whole bloody massacre for upload to every news network and social media site, where it would hopefully go viral.

In hours, days at most, the resulting shit storm would engulf the Arcane Corps as people started asking why the military was turning mentally unstable Feral veterans loose in small towns.

That would quickly grow into a Category Five political hurricane when it came out the Corps was running missions in Ukraine, despite the risk of triggering a nuclear war. The scandal could force the American government to pull its support from Ukraine, which should then fall to the Russian army within weeks.

The trick, of course, would be surviving this operation. It was almost impossible to control a berserk Feral without a high-powered automatic weapon, and she had no interest in becoming a martyr. Anastasia wouldn't even be in here if the video she was shooting hadn't been crucial to the plan.

She'd just have to sing to the psychotic bitch with every ounce of her considerable Bard Talent and pray to God it worked.

Either way, orders were orders -- and Anastasia had no intention of using the back of her head to catch bullets.

* * *

Grant glowered at his laptop. His eyes were gritty from lack of sleep from working both Jimmy's shift and his own.

All I have to do is get through the rest of my shift, and Baker will...

His door slammed open. Startled, he looked up to see records clerk Deb Kelly in the doorway, though she'd just headed out to lunch. "Chief, I was headed to the Spoon when I heard gunfire. Sounded like an active shooter. Margay's tiger is roaring and people are screaming."

Shit! He catapulted out of his seat as Deb ducked out of his way. "Call dispatch and have them send backup!"

Grant bolted down the station's narrow hall, past the tiny jail they used as a drunk tank, and up the short flight of stairs to the street where his Ford Police Interceptor SUV waited. He hit the fob, jerked the door open and threw himself inside.

Margay! he thought, heart hammering as he started the SUV, threw the unit into drive and stomped the gas. He hit lights and sirens, the SUV's tires squealing as it rocketed up the street toward Main. "Ashburg I-1, shots fired at 415 Main Street, officer needs assistance."

Barely slowing at the light, he blasted across the intersection to skid the SUV to a halt blocking the street. People streamed from the restaurant to run in all directions as he threw the door open and piled out, drawing his weapon. Margay's tiger roared, the sound chilling.

"What's happening?" he yelled at the middle-aged couple running past.

"Margay's gone crazy!" the man shouted back. "Her tiger's loose!"

"What about the shooter?"

"There is no shooter!"

Raz roared, the sound impossibly loud as someone else ran out the restaurant door. *Shit, she sounds pissed*. He raced across the sidewalk, then slowed to peer through the plate glass window. Charging inside blind was a good way to get dead.

The glowing tiger crouched in the middle of the Spoon's dining room, ears pinned back, tail lashing, snarling at Jocelyn. Margay's mother stood planted between Raz and those who hadn't yet gotten the hell out. Even through the glass, he could hear the cat's chilling snarl.

Oh, that's not good. I've got to get these people out of there before she kills somebody.

Slowly, carefully, Grant pulled the door open and slid inside.

* * *

The reek of black powder mixed with magic and the nauseating scent of burning herbs flooded Margay's nose, making her head spin. One minute she was in the Spoon's dining area. The next, she fought to contain the deadly bloom of the bomb trying to rip her apart. Screams and reeking smoke surrounded her, and she had no idea where she was.

"Baby, you're okay." Margay knew that voice -- it was Mama. But that made no sense. Mom wasn't in Ukraine... *I must not be in Ukraine.*

But then the smoke rolled over her again, stinking of magic, and a searing, white-hot blast of pain pounded her consciousness, threatening to snuff her like a candle.

The world wrenched sideways, and a Caliphate Feral lion tore at Raz's manifestation with fangs and claws as she tried to keep him out of a classroom full of Afghan girls. He was bigger -- twice as big as Raz at least -- and the glowing beast's jaws clamped her throat...

"Baby, you're all right. Nobody's shooting at us. It was just a prank..."

Mama. That's Mama...

But when she inhaled to speak, smoke flooded her head and fire engulfed her yet again. *It hurt, hurt so fucking bad, and they were dying -- the traitorous son of a bitch had* killed *them.*

Razia roared in fury and gathered herself to spring…

But her mother's voice floated out of the swirling smoke again. "It's all right, honey. Everything's fine…"

Raz snarled.

No. This isn't… We're not in Charivnyk. We're back home, Raz. It's Mama.

But the smoke rolled, and fire raged in her body, tearing her apart again. And the traitor was right *there*.

Right in front of her!

"No, baby, it's me…"

* * *

Shit, Grant thought, watching the glowing tiger snarl up at Margay's mother. Jocelyn looked small and fragile compared to her daughter's boiling glow. Just beyond her stood his mother, Nancy Sawyer, who'd worked for Jocelyn as a waitress since his father had walked out on them when Grant was nine. Mom was dead white, green eyes huge in her bloodless face.

Whatever the hell had happened had set Margay off so badly, she didn't recognize her mom at all.

"It's all right, Margay," Jocelyn crooned, voice soothing despite the terror in her wide brown eyes. "I'm *okay. You're okay*. Nobody shot at us. It was just firecrackers. Some jerk kid playing a prank. Everything's fine. It was just a box full of fireworks. That's all. I know it sounded like the battle of Falluja, but it was just fireworks."

Jocelyn's gaze lifted to meet Grant's as he edged in the door, gun drawn. Her eyes widened at the sight of his weapon, and she shook her head at him, silently begging him not to shoot.

Don't worry, Jos, I'm not that stupid. Grant had worked with Ferals when he'd been with the Laurel

Sheriff's department, and he knew a big predator manifestation was the next best thing to bulletproof. It would take sustained fire from an AR-15 -- or a rocket-propelled grenade -- to punch through it. Not that he wanted to shoot Margay with either.

Slowly, Grant holstered his weapon and spared a glance for the nearest booth. A five-year-old sobbed in the protective clutch of her mother, who lay atop her under the table, trying to shield the child with her own body. The woman stared at him over the little girl's dark head, her gaze pleading, her face dead pale.

Keeping his voice low and calm, just loud enough to be heard over Raz's growls, Grant murmured to the woman, "It's time to leave. Don't run. If you run, her instinct will be to chase you. Just move slowly. Take your time."

The woman nodded jerkily and climbed to her feet, staring nervously at the tiger. When she was on her feet, she bent, extending shaking hands. The little girl leaped into them, wrapping her arms and legs around her in a desperate, panicked clutch.

Grant reached to open the door for her, and the pair tiptoed out, both stealing nervous glances back at Raz.

He turned, saw something glowing beneath one of the booths, and realized it was a cell phone. The woman had it aimed at Margay.

You've got to be fucking kidding me.

* * *

Anastasia was still shooting video when the police chief bent to glare under the table at her. "What the hell are you doing?" he hissed. "If you don't get out of here *now*, you're going to live-stream yourself getting eaten."

She suppressed a snarl. *But the stupid* bliatz *hasn't eaten* anybody *yet. The potion hadn't worked.*

Realizing she was drawing attention she didn't need, Anastasia thumbed the video app off and slid out from under the table. She skittered out of the restaurant, relieved despite herself. She'd dared the devil more than once for Russian military intelligence, but this op was something else again.

Still, she'd watch. See if the *bliatz* finally lost it. *We've got to get that video…*

*   *   *

Karl had found a good location where the painted sign on the Mama's Spoon window didn't obscure his view of the dining room. That gave the tiny camera set on the forehead of his mask an excellent view of the bloodshed.

Assuming blood actually *was* shed, anyway.

When Anastasia had left the restaurant among the panicking customers, he'd headed across the street to take her place. While he was busy, she'd keep an eye on the American *durak*. Though they intended to make Austin the fall guy if they got caught, Karl was beginning to hope that wouldn't be necessary. He badly wanted to kill the arrogant *yobanyi karas'* himself. It would be tricky, given Czar, but nothing got Karl's blood up like a challenging kill.

Now he stared through the window with closed eyes, watching the play of magic. Judging by the glitter in the darkness, the fireworks had done their job, spraying the potion throughout the dining room.

Yet the tiger just stood there, rumbling in threat. Why wasn't the little *suka* going after her mother? With all that potion in her system, she shouldn't even know it *was* her mother.

If they'd dosed that *zasranees*, Austin, with the same drug, he'd have already butchered everyone in the restaurant. When they'd been prepping, Karl had even made plans about how to get Anastasia out before the cat could kill her. Yet the tiger hadn't attacked *anyone*.

Just our luck, Karl thought in disgust. The girl Austin had sworn would lose her shit in the first five minutes turned out to have a will of iron. They should have known better than to listen to that *pidaras*. Austin's dick did far too much of his thinking.

Killing him was beginning to sound better all the time. Maybe they wouldn't even need a fall guy.

Karl sighed. Unfortunately, Anastasia was a stickler for orders. And she outranked him.

* * *

The tiger didn't appear to notice when Grant and Nancy got the last of the customers out of the restaurant. Raz was laser-focused on Jocelyn, ears laid flat, muzzle twisted in a snarl, gold eyes blazing as her tail flick flick flicked like the pendulum of a clock. *I've got to do something. I can't let her kill her mother. Jocelyn's all she's got left.*

"Where's the rest of the staff?" he asked his mother softly as Nancy edged closer to him.

"Went out the back," she breathed, referring to employee parking behind the restaurant.

"Think you can get out of here?"

But when she tried to move toward the door, Raz's head snapped toward her with a snarl. Nancy froze, green eyes going so wide, the whites showed.

I'm going to have to distract Raz to give the Moms a chance to escape. "Margay," Grant said softly, lifting both hands as he stepped closer to the cat. She snarled louder, and he went still. "Hey, Margay, it's me --

Grant." He took another slow step.

Raz tensed.

A bead of sweat rolled down his spine. His mouth went dry, and he licked his lips. "I'm not going to hurt you, baby. You *know* me. Remember we used to play Arcane Corps out in the woods? I was always the Arcanist and you were the big cat Feral."

Raz stopped snarling to stare intently at him. Her flattened ears began to lift.

If he concentrated, he could just make out Margay within the manifestation's glow. She seemed to be floating inside the shell of her tiger like something out of a science fiction movie. Her face looked strained through the magical shimmer, as if struggling to hear something just beyond audible range. "Remember when we went to prom? You wore that long gold silk dress with a slit. You were so" -- *everything I could never have because you're magic and I'm not* --"beautiful."

Raz straightened out of her crouch and her ears pricked. Her muzzle began to relax out of that terrifying snarl.

"Why don't you come out, Margay?" he suggested, keeping his voice deep and low. "You don't need your manifestation. Everything's okay. I won't let anything happen to you. None of this is your fault."

"Grant?" Margay's voice sounded far away and a little ragged, as if she spoke from a dream. Or a nightmare. "Grant, I… I *died*. The bomb went off and we died. He killed us."

Bomb? "Who's 'he?'"

"It wasn't a bomb, sweetheart," Jocelyn broke in. "It was just fireworks. Somebody's idea of a prank."

Grant frowned. Every Fourth of July, public service announcements warned people that fireworks could trigger veterans with PTSD. Everybody in town knew Margay was a combat vet. What fucking idiot would play a prank like this on a vet *with a tiger? I'm going to find out who did this and charge their ass. After I kick them first. Hard.*

"Mama?" Margay peered at her through the manifestation. "There was a bomb. He killed me. It would've killed everybody, but it just killed me."

Wait, what?

"That wasn't a bomb, baby," Jocelyn told her, her voice warm and soothing. "That was just some kid's prank. You're home now, and you're safe. Why don't you let your manifestation go? You don't need it -- we're all fine. It was just a prank."

"Mom?" She sounded confused.

"Yes, baby, it's me."

"Oh, hell," Margay said in a completely different voice that sounded like someone who'd woken from a nightmare. The glowing tiger vanished, and she slumped to the floor, shaking. "God, oh God, *shit!* I'm so sorry! I heard you scream, and I thought... And I smelled RDX and I thought we were trying to contain that bomb again..."

Contain the bomb 'again?' What the hell is she talking about? Grant shot a questioning glance at Jocelyn, who shrugged, just as confused as he was.

Apparently, he wasn't the only one Margay had kept in the dark.

Grant was just beginning to relax when he heard the high-pitched shriek of approaching sirens. Horror iced his blood as he imagined SWAT charging into the restaurant.

Chapter Three

The last thing we need is a gang of trigger-happy deputies drawing on Margay just as we got her calmed down. Grant grabbed the radio handset clipped to his shoulder epaulet and said, "Ashburg I-1, I've got the situation under control. Backup is no longer necessary."

Jocelyn knelt beside her daughter and slid an arm around her. "Why don't we have some tea? I have some of the chamomile potion made up."

Margay tried to stand, but her knees buckled. Grant caught her elbows before she hit the ground again. He frowned at her, worried. "Can you walk? Are you hurt anywhere?"

"I'm okay," she said, sounding a little dazed. "It was just... just a really bad... bad flashback."

She leaned into him, her body feeling surprisingly light against his. Margay had lost too much of the solid muscle she'd come home with. *I wonder just how many four a.m. runs she's been doing?*

Wrapping an arm around her waist, he half-carried, half-led her to the nearest booth. Tried not to notice the soft pressure of her breast against his arm. *God, holding her feels good...*

As her mom hurried into the kitchen to brew the potion, Margay looked at him, her eyes vague and vulnerable. "What happened?"

"You manifested."

Her eyes rounded in dismay. "Were you... Were you here for lunch?"

He shook his head. "My records clerk heard Raz roar and what she thought was gunfire. Mom and I got everybody out of the restaurant."

Margay looked sick. "I manifested in front of the customers?"

He winced. "Yes."

"Noooo," she moaned, burying her face in her hands. "This is a nightmare. I've been afraid I'd do this. I can't believe I manifested in front of half the people in town."

Grant hesitated, then knelt beside the booth and put a hand on her knee. Her leg quivered under his palm, muscles vibrating with stress. "You didn't hurt anybody. That's the important thing."

She dropped her hands to look at him, golden eyes worried. "Are you sure? I'm not smelling blood, but…"

He smiled. "Positive. Raz never touched anybody -- just crouched and growled."

"Thank God for small mercies." She sighed. "It could have been worse."

While he was struggling to come up with something soothing to say, his mother called, "Hey, Grant, take a look at this."

Frowning, he glanced up. Nancy stood behind the checkout counter, looking down at the floor, plump fists planted on her wide hips. She wore the restaurant uniform of black chinos, a black Spoon T, and a red apron wrapped around her waist. Her messy blonde bun was half collapsed down her back.

Thank God she wasn't hurt. "What?"

She didn't look up, still glowering at the floor. "This… doesn't look right."

Grant shot Margay a glance, decided he could leave her alone a few minutes, and went to join his mother. She pointed at the floor. "What do you think of that?"

There was a seared patch of soot on the floor

behind the counter. Shreds of what looked like blackened white cardboard lay scattered around the soot patch, along with the burned remains of firecrackers. Another streak of soot extended six feet up the wall.

Instinctively, he caught his mother's elbow and pulled her with him as he stepped away to avoid stepping on the evidence.

The smell of gunpowder hung in the air, along with another scent he didn't recognize -- an odd, burned vegetable smell. Something herbal and a little dank, something like pot, but… not quite.

"You said this was fireworks?" Grant crouched, spotting a larger chunk of singed white cardboard that appeared bent. A box flap? "Is that part of a box?"

His mother tilted her head, considering. "Looks like it was a bakery box."

Grant frowned as he studied the debris. "They put burning firecrackers in a cardboard box? Why didn't it go off in their hands?" He bent lower, but the bottom of the counter was flush with the floor -- there was no room for anything to roll beneath it.

His mom lifted her brows at him. "You're asking *me*? Aren't *you* the detective?"

"Yeah, and something about this doesn't smell like a prank." He eyed the remnants of the fireworks, then pulled out his cell and started taking photos.

Grant rose and began a fast, dirty search of the room, kneeling to check under booths and tables, snapping pictures with his iPhone of anything that didn't belong. There were a few shreds of paper thrown farther than he would have expected, but most of it lay on and around the counter.

What he didn't see was any sign of wires or anything that might be a detonator. *Were* they ordinary firecrackers? *How did the bastard set them off?*

Instinct niggled at him -- the feeling he'd often gotten as a Laurel County detective when he'd found something significant. He rose to his feet, and held the cell to his mouth. "Hey, Siri, call CSI."

There was no answer at the Ash County Sheriff's Office forensics unit, so he left a message. Hopefully they'd get back to him -- the unit was seriously understaffed.

He turned to Nancy. "Did you see anyone bring in the box?"

His mother shook her head, wrinkles pleating around her green eyes. "I didn't even *see* a box. I stepped behind the counter to answer the phone, and I'd swear there was no box back there. The caller asked for Jocelyn, so I called her to the phone. But the minute she answered, he hung up on her -- and all *hell* broke loose. I thought for a minute there we had a mass shooter."

Yeah, something's definitely off. "I think," Grant said slowly, "I need to treat this like a crime scene. Which means we all need to get out of here until the scene can be processed for evidence." He turned to Jocelyn, who'd returned with a teapot and a mug for her daughter. "Mind if we go upstairs and talk? I need to interview all three of you."

Jocelyn blinked. "Is that necessary? I mean, this was a prank, right?"

"Maybe. Maybe not." He paused, processing. "Come to think of it, I need to interview everyone who was in the restaurant. Which means I'm going to need a list."

Nancy frowned. "I'll try to remember, but they all left without paying their checks, so we don't have register receipts."

He shrugged. "We'll have to do the best we can."

As Grant escorted his mother, Jocelyn, and Margay out of the Spoon, Officer Roger Porter pulled up in his patrol car. The big, graying cop got out of the SUV and eyed him with parental concern.

Roger had the beefy face and heavy shoulders of a former football player who'd run a bit to seed. Now in his late fifties, he'd been a cop when Grant was in diapers. At first, he'd been a little dubious of his new chief, but he'd come around. Now there was genuine worry on his face. "Hell, chief, are you all right? Did we have injuries?"

"Not so far as I know. Margay's cat manifested, but she didn't attack anybody. Still, with everybody running…" He shrugged.

"No thanks to you, Roger," Jocelyn snapped. "Where were you, anyway?"

The big cop looked startled. She wasn't normally bitchy with people, but an adrenaline jag tended to do that, especially when you weren't used to it. Any other cop would have cut Jocelyn off at the knees, but Roger had been her husband's best friend. "I was halfway to the county jail with a prisoner when the call went out."

"When you've got a prisoner in the car, you can't respond to other calls," Grant told her. "You have to get them into a cell first." He turned to Roger. "Put up the crime scene tape and keep an eye on the Spoon. Hopefully the forensics unit will grace us with their presence."

"On it," Roger said, and turned back to his SUV to get the tape out of the rear.

Now all Grant had to do was figure out what the hell was going on.

* * *

Grant followed Margay, Nancy and Jocelyn up to the Whitfields' apartment. He hadn't visited since Darrell's death, so he looked around. They'd redecorated since his last visit.

Jocelyn always decorated for Christmas, so he wasn't surprised to see the seven-foot tree blinking cheerfully where it would be visible through one of the tall arched windows. A black glass entertainment center stood nearby, a huge flat-screen TV hanging above that.

Facing them was a new U-shaped dove-gray sectional with high rolled arms and back, along with a matching coffee table.

The space flowed into Jocelyn's kitchen, which had been renovated with stainless-steel appliances -- probably with *Magical Kitchens* money -- set against the building's exposed red brick walls. The cabinetry was white, with white marble countertops that gleamed mutely in the dim light. Pots of fresh herbs hung from the ceiling or tucked into nooks equipped with grow lights.

Beyond that lay the same dining room table he recognized from childhood, though the sleigh and reindeer centerpiece was new. Grant and Nancy took seats at the table as Margay slid into a chair and slumped there, eyes closed. Her mother bustled around making both a pot of coffee and her migraine-fighting tea.

Jocelyn finally put a cup down in front of her daughter, who dumped Splenda into it and downed it with the grim determination of someone drinking a laxative.

As Jocelyn served coffee and offered around a plate of Christmas cookies, Grant asked, "Mind if I interview Mom in your office?"

She frowned, looking a little uneasy, as if she were worried what he intended. "Interview her?"

It stung that Jocelyn distrusted him, but he ignored the stab of hurt. "You're all witnesses," he explained patiently. "I need to interview you separately. If this is more than a prank, I've got to follow procedure."

"Oh. Sure, go ahead."

He and Nancy picked up their coffee mugs and headed into the apartment's spare bedroom, now used as an office. Unlike the kitchen, it looked no different than it had when Grant and Margay used to game there after school.

He watched his mother drop into the chair in front of Jocelyn's desktop, then sat at the other desk, where a laptop stood open. Grant activated his phone's recording app and identified them both for the recording.

"I'm going to have to repeat some of the questions I asked downstairs to get them on the record. Tell me exactly what happened. First, where did the box come from?"

Nancy frowned. "No idea. I never saw it. Not in one piece, anyway."

"So you didn't notice anyone bring it in?"

"Nope, but we were pretty busy." She shrugged. "Maybe Brenda did."

Brenda Hollings was the other waitress. "Where's she?"

"Probably went out the back door with the rest of the crew. I can text you her contact info."

"That would be helpful. So what happened before the fireworks went off?"

"I was taking an order when the phone rang. There was a man on the line. He asked to speak to

Jocelyn about a catering job, and I said she was busy -- we were in the middle of the lunch crowd." She pursed her lips thoughtfully. "But it could be a coincidence. He didn't sound like the kind of guy who'd do something like this. Didn't sound like he was from around here either."

"Where did he sound like he was from?"

"Brooklyn, maybe -- he had that kind of accent. He definitely wasn't a local." She frowned. "His name was... Richard? No, Robert. Robert Ford."

Grant went on alert. "Ford? You sure about that?"

"Yeah, why..." Her eyes widened. "You think he's related to that terrorist you busted?"

Virgil and Indigo Ford had been a pair of Talent terrorists who'd murdered Fred Briggs, a Feral who'd run a big cat sanctuary in Laurel County. Grant had investigated the Briggs case when he'd been a detective with the Laurel County Sheriff's Office.

Virgil, a polar bear Feral, and Indigo, his Arcanist wife, had committed a whole series of sacrificial murders to fuel a death magic spell that would have assassinated the U.S. President and every member of Congress. They'd also massacred cops and civilians at Faraday Square. Grant, who'd been there at the time, still had nightmares all these years later.

Was this incident related to that? Grant considered the idea, then shook his head. "If he was, he wouldn't have given his name. But it might have been some asshole's way of getting cute. Can you remember exactly what he said?"

Nancy frowned, her blonde brows pleating as if she were struggling to remember. "He said he was looking for an Alchemist chef to cater his daughter's wedding, and he'd seen Jocelyn on *Magical Kitchens*."

"That show is the gift that keeps on giving. Then what did he say?"

"The wedding was going to be a big event in Columbia in the spring, and he wanted to make sure it was something special. But if Jocelyn didn't want the job, he'd find somebody else. I gathered if she didn't talk to him, the offer was off."

"What happened then?"

"I called Jocelyn to the phone, and the guy hung up on her. She slammed down the handset and all hell broke loose. I thought we had a mass shooter until I saw the light from the firecrackers going off and realized what was happening. Jocelyn screamed -- I think one of them burned her -- and then Margay came barreling through the kitchen doors." She sighed and raked both hands through her graying blond hair, and her face crumpled into tears. "Grant, I don't think I've ever been that fuckin' scared. And that includes when your dad was at his worst."

"Yeah, I was scared too." She was right. They'd come entirely too close. *I almost lost Mom, Jocelyn* and *Margay. And why the fireworks? Given everyone knew combat vets had an issue with firecrackers…*

Had this attack been targeted *at* Margay? Or at Jocelyn?

What the hell was going on?

* * *

"The fucking potion didn't work," Austin's voice growled from empty air as they walked the four blocks back to the house they'd rented. "She breathed it in, but she still didn't kill anybody. Hell, sometimes it's all I can do not to kill *you*."

Anastasia was tempted to tell him that said more about his control than the potion, but she batted down the impulse. Austin might be an idiot, but with that cat of his, he could still be a *useful* idiot. "The potion was not the problem."

"Keep cat to yourself," rumbled Karl, also still invisible. "Have to drop manifestation sometime -- and I'll be waiting." Karl had always been rather protective where Anastasia was concerned. She probably shouldn't have slept with him. *He might be tempting, but he was too complicated.*

"But the plan --"

"It doesn't matter," she interrupted. "The video we shot is enough, especially if I give the locals a little encouragement. These Norms have been marinating in conspiracy theories for years. It won't take much to set them off."

* * *

By the time Grant and Nancy emerged from the home office, Margay had finished her tea. She looked calmer and more alert, and he decided it was a good time to talk to her mother. "Hey, Jocelyn -- I've got some questions for you too."

"Sure." She gave him a smile, but it looked a little tight. Probably worrying about the repercussions of today's little adventure. "Want some more coffee? I've made another pot."

Jocelyn's coffee beat the fuck out of Starbucks. "I'd love some."

As she poured him a cup and added more to her own, she said, "Nancy…"

"I'll sit with Margay."

Margay looked up, shamefaced. "That's not necessary. I'm feeling better and Raz has mellowed out."

"Glad to hear it," Nancy said, studying her. "But

you still look like you have a headache. Want some PowerUp?" The drink contained electrolytes and a mild potion designed to help Talents recover from the backlash of using their magic.

Margay forced a smile. "Sounds good. But I can get it…"

Grant followed Jocelyn and the coffee into her home office. As she handed him his mug, he asked, "Is it okay if I record this?"

"No problem. What do you need to know?"

"What did that caller say when you answered the phone?"

"Nothing. The minute I said hello, I heard a click. A heartbeat later, the fireworks went off."

He took a thoughtful sip of his coffee. She'd added the precise amount of sugar and cream he liked. Which, given it was Jocelyn, didn't surprise him in the least. "Did you notice a bakery box when you went behind the counter?"

"Bakery box?" She frowned at him over her own coffee.

"When I examined the site where the fireworks went off, I found the remains of what Mom said looked like a bakery box. I think the fireworks must have been in that box."

Jocelyn frowned. "But… How did they set them off? Was there a detonator?"

"No idea. I didn't see anything that looked like a trigger. Did anybody bring a bakery box into the restaurant?"

"I don't know. I was in the kitchen."

"Did you notice the box when you went to the phone? It would have been behind the counter."

"No… Oh, wait." Jocelyn frowned, her graying brows knitting, the wrinkles around her brown eyes deepening in a squint. "When I reached to take the phone, my foot kicked something on the floor. I looked down, but there was nothing there."

"Nothing at all?"

"Nope. I figured I must have kicked the wall, but it was about two feet away. Then I hung up, and it sounded like Pearl Harbor went off right beside me. Something hurt my thigh -- a graze from one of the fireworks. Burned right through my pants leg. I yelled, and Margay came running in her mani. That's when I realized we had a real problem." She paused and took another long sip, thinking. "Grant, I noticed something when I was trying to talk Margay down. The air smelled like black powder from the fireworks, but there was something else to it too. Something herbal. Now that I think about it, it smelled a little like marijuana, along with fennel, cinnamon, saffron, and anise -- which can be hallucinogenic in high doses -- and magic to amplify and target the effect. I know Alchemist magic when I taste or smell it, and that was definitely Alc magic." She paused, considering. "When I closed my eyes to look at Margay, I could see some kind of magical dust glittering in the smoke."

"You think it was a potion?"

She paused, sipping her coffee before she nodded slowly. "And I think it must have been aimed at Margay. I've seen her deal with flashbacks before -- she had one just this morning, and it took me about five minutes to bring her out of it. She was sleepwalking, so I was a little worried, but I wasn't really scared. Her daddy had PTSD sleepwalking episodes, but he never hurt me either. This afternoon was different. Her reaction was so extreme, I was genuinely afraid. Margay would normally never hurt me. If that potion contained a drug designed to set her off, that would explain her reaction."

"But wouldn't a potion affect everybody who breathed it in? Nobody else seemed affected."

"Depends on the potion. Powerful Talents are more sensitive to magic, and Margay is powerful as hell. I'm nowhere near as strong as she is, and I did feel a little weird at the time -- afraid, but also a little..." She frowned, lips pursing. "Floaty, like my head didn't quite touch my shoulders, you know?"

"I was just scared shitless."

She snorted. "Me too. Could be I *was* affected, but her reaction was stronger than mine. Norms might not have felt it at all."

"Or you might have just been scared. Assuming it was some kind of spell, who do you think would have cast it? Do you have enemies?"

"Me? No. Margay? Half the Middle East, plus whoever Uncle Sam's been sending her to mess with since the wars ended."

"But what the fuck are they doing in Ashburg, SC?" When one graying brow lifted in cool disapproval, he realized what he'd said and winced. "Sorry about that, Ms. Whitfield."

"I know your mama raised you better."

Grant grinned. "And so did you." He drained the last of the coffee, enjoying the warm glow anything she made always gave him. "I think I'll go have a word with Margay. Can you and Mom make a list of the customers on scene today? Including descriptions of anyone you didn't recognize."

"We can try."

* * *

Margay and Nancy put their heads together about who they'd seen in the dining room before the

MEED went off, then handed the resulting list off to Grant. Jocelyn wasn't saying much, obviously still worrying about the effect the incident would have on both her daughter and her restaurant.

As if sensing her uneasiness, Nancy gave Jocelyn a thoughtful look. "Let's go get dinner and drinks in Laurelton. There's this new Alchemist restaurant I've been dying to try…"

Jocelyn shot her daughter a look. "I don't know…"

Margay drained the last of her PowerUp and sighed. "Mom, I'm feeling much better. I think I can survive you and Nancy going to lunch." She lifted a brow. "I did survive ten years in the Middle East -- despite the best efforts of the Caliphate."

Her mother studied her, frowning. Margay stared back, her gaze steady.

As if realizing her obvious doubts weren't building her daughter's confidence, Jocelyn sighed. "Given that we aren't going to be able to clean the Spoon until CSI gets done, a trip to Laurelton isn't a bad idea. And yes, I was curious about that restaurant too."

Fifteen minutes later, as the door closed behind the two women, it hit Grant.

We're alone now.

* * *

Margay was acutely aware of Grant's warm masculine scent. She licked her lips and blurted the first thing that came to mind. "Have you had lunch? We've got leftovers from last night. Roast, corn on the cob, and green beans. Now that the backlash headache's gone, I'm starved."

"I never turn down your mom's cooking." He

grinned, humor lighting his vivid green eyes.

For a moment their gazes caught, and heat rolled through her, made even hotter by memories that made her pulse leap. He'd been a devoted lover even in high school. How much better would he be as a grown man? Her throat went dry. *Bad idea, Margay. Bad. He doesn't need my crazy. And I don't need his… everything.*

Raz chuffed in her head, not buying her bullshit any more than she did.

While she started preparing the leftovers, Grant called dispatch and went 10-7 for lunch. Then he asked if she'd seen anyone bring in a bakery box.

"I didn't notice anything while I was bussing tables, but that doesn't mean much. I was mostly busy in the kitchen." She went to work cutting slices of roast as her stomach growled.

Without being asked, Grant started setting the table as he explained about the caller hanging up on her mother.

She popped the first loaded plate into the microwave to reheat. "Sounds like someone was trying to get Mama close to that box. The Caliphate used to pull the same crap when they wanted to lure victims into the blast radius of a MEED." Magically Enhanced Explosive Devices had been the bane of civilians and the American military in both Afghanistan and Iraq.

He leaned a hip against the counter and studied her. "So you think they were targeting your mother?"

"No, I think she's right -- they were targeting *me*." The microwave dinged and she handed the plate to Grant and put her own in.

He put the plate down, then reached into the fridge for another bottle of PowerUp and handed it to her. But as he grabbed a Coke for himself, he froze, embarrassment in his eyes. "Damn, I took this without asking. Sorry."

She gave him an amused look. "Like you're not as much my mama's kid as I am."

He flashed her a grin and took a sip of his Coke. "And my mom has always felt the same about you." He studied her over the can, his clever green eyes probing in that handsome face. Seeing way too much. "Why are you so convinced someone's targeting you instead of Jocelyn?"

"If we're right, this involves at least an Arcanist, which isn't a cheap Talent to buy." She leaned a hip against the counter and watched the plate revolve in the microwave. "Not the kind of money you spend to mess with somebody who runs a restaurant. Why not just shoot her or burn the Spoon down? Simpler and cheaper." The thought of her mother dead made her tense. Raz seconded that with a low rumble and some truly gory images.

"One of the Humanists in the Adrian Flemming case ran a restaurant," Grant pointed out. "He was pissed because an Alchemist diner was eating into his business."

The microwave dinged, and Margay pulled out her plate, grimacing a little at the heat. As they headed for the table, she said, "Again, that stunt today was too elaborate. These guys must have used some kind of invisibility spell to keep anyone from spotting that box. You need to have CSI check the box remains with a black light to check for sigils in ultraviolet paint."

"Yeah, I left them a message about that." He lifted a brow as they sat down. "I have worked Arc cases before."

Margay grinned. "Big ones, too. Hell, President Roth resigned over the Flemming thing. I was in Afghanistan, but Mom sent me links to the news stories. She and Nancy were *so* proud."

"They didn't get the death threats." His eyes widened. "Do *not* mention that to the moms."

"Yeah, I'm right there with you. I'd rather Mama didn't know ninety percent of the shit I did."

They were silent for a few moments as they ate. "I doubt the crime scene guys will find anything," Margay said at last, taking a sip of her PowerUp. "You've got to be lucky as hell to pull sigils off an exploded MEED, because the explosion is strongest near the spell. But there was definitely magic involved. I suspect it was more to render the box invisible than amplify the explosion. Otherwise there wouldn't have been anything left of the Spoon." For an instant, an image flashed through her mind -- the wreckage of a wedding celebration a suicide bomber had hit, the twisted, charred bodies among the remains of tables and chairs.

If today's MEED had been designed to do worse than set her off... In her mind, Raz's growl grew louder. She heard a *scriiiitch* and glanced down to see she'd manifested glowing claws and was absently raking them over the table, leaving grooves in the varnish. Her inner ten-year-old froze. *Mom's going to kill me.*

"Uh, Margay..."

"Yeah, sorry." She banished the claws.

He gave her a grin and said, obviously trying to lighten the mood, "Seemed like *all* your furniture had claw marks when we were growing up."

She laughed, remembering. "Mama kept threatening to buy Daddy a scratching post." They ate in silence for a few moments. "You know, whoever planted that box must have been wearing a Spook Suit. Otherwise, someone would have seen them."

He nodded slowly. "Makes sense. But... How common are Spook Suits?"

She shrugged. "The military uses them, and so do some CIA agents overseas, but possessing one is illegal for anybody else under federal law. They're also seriously expensive magical tech, so not something your average Humanist redneck is going to have access to."

"Your mom seems to think there was a potion in the box of fireworks. She believes it was targeted at you."

Margay nodded. "She's probably right. I could still scent traces of it even after I shook off the effects. Smelled like fennel, cinnamon and magic." She paused, considering it. "Maybe some anise. And weed. Definitely weed."

"Mmm." Grant put down his fork. "When you first came out of it, you said something about a bomb and that 'he' had killed you. I had the impression you were talking about when Raz died. Who is 'he?' Could this be the same guy?"

Margay stared at him, her jaw dropping. "Wait, what? I don't remember saying that." She shook her head. "Must have been one strong hallucinogen in that smoke."

The idea sent a chill through her as she remembered the confusing storm of impressions -- the way she'd first thought she was back at the Charivnyk base enclosure, then believed she was at the girl's school bombing in Afghanistan. The psychic whiplash produced by the drug had been so terrifying, she'd almost lost control of Raz completely.

With her mother standing *three feet away*. With Grant. "I could have *killed* you today. I could've killed my mother -- *both* our mothers." The words came out low and hoarse, strained with the effort at self-control when all she wanted was to scream.

And she would have, if ten years of war hadn't taught her that she couldn't afford such self-indulgence. "It's like… hell has followed me home and is trying to destroy everyone I love, and I'm afraid that I'm just going to lose it and…"

Grant made a low sound and rose, circling the table to pull her to her feet and wrap his arms around her. Throat tight, she let herself sink into the strength and warmth of his body. He wasn't that much taller than she was -- not like Austin -- but he was solid in a way Austin hadn't been, for all her ex's size and bodybuilder brawn.

Grant was the human equivalent of a thick cement wall in a firefight, bullets thudding around you as the wounded screamed. He made her feel… safe.

Margay wrapped her arms more tightly around his muscled torso. Found the courage to admit what she hadn't been able to say to her mother. "I'm so goddamn afraid I won't be able to save any of you." She took a deep breath and spoke her nightmare out loud. "Or worse, that I'll be the one to kill you."

Chapter Four

"You won't. You wouldn't," Grant said, calm and low and sure. There was no doubt whatsoever in either his words or his tone. Drinking in his scent, she found no deception either. Yes, there was a trace of fear, but she sensed he wasn't afraid of her, but *for* her.

"Margay, they gave you a drug today that was supposed to make you kill your mother, me, and as many other people as possible." He drew back to meet her gaze, his own level, sure. *"But you didn't do it.* Somehow you held on, kept fighting. You fought the drug and the flashbacks and your own PTSD. And you *won."* Those broad, familiar hands cupped either side of her face in warmth. "You've always been so goddamn strong, even before you got your cat."

"Yeah, but…"

"But nothing. Remember that guidance counselor? The one who told you you'd never get into the Corps, and if you did, the best you could hope for was to be a dog handler, because…"

"…'The Corps doesn't do affirmative action.'" An unwilling laugh escaped her. "That bastard got me through Basic. When they turned the dogs loose on me in training and I thought I was kibble, I remembered Mr. Talley. No way in hell was I going to give that jerk the satisfaction of failing. So I wrapped my power around those mastiffs and made them *want* to obey me. Like Dad always said…"

"'Nothing's as motivating as making a bigot eat his words.'" He shook his head. "Damn, I miss him."

Her throat tightened. "So do I. Especially now."

"He'd be so fucking proud of you." Green gaze intense, Grant brushed his thumbs back and forth across her cheeks. "Because you did it. You beat the odds *and* the misogynists in the Corps."

"To be fair, there is some logic to the policy," she said. "Male Ferals weigh more, and their muscle mass gives them more leverage when they're trying to use their Familiar's strength. The problem is, Afghan women wouldn't even *speak* to American men, so the Corps decided they needed women on the teams."

"Yeah, but that's not the only reason they picked you. When push came to shove, when you were sucking in hallucinogens and having a PTSD flashback, you fought it off. I've been in some terrifying situations -- the Faraday Square Massacre leaps to mind --"

"Yeah, that was impressively nasty even by Corps standards."

" -- So I *do* know how hard it is to function when a frickin' polar bear is eating cops twenty feet away. I still have nightmares about trying to shoot through the bear's manifestation with an AR-15 without killing that deputy. Then there was that fucking Humanist riot when half the rednecks in upstate South Carolina tried to beat in my face. *Nothing's* as terrifying as a riot."

"It looked it." Margay had seen video of both incidents, and they'd scared the living hell out of her at how close he'd come to dying. "At least I have magic. You didn't."

"Yeah, but my point is, *you held it together today.*"

"This time."

"This time, next time -- *every* time. Because I know you. Remember when those four little pricks caught us walking home from school when we were in… What, fifth grade?"

"Fourth."

"I thought I was going have to defend you…"

She grinned, remembering the way he'd plowed

into the boy who'd been two years older and twenty pounds heavier. "You did."

"But you did just as much damage. You fought for me, and I fought for you. And I'll fight for you the next time, just as I know you'll fight for me -- including against your own demons. Because that's who you are."

He believes in me. Something about that thought made the tensed muscles of her shoulders relax. Her gaze dropped to his lush mouth, and she licked lips that had suddenly gone dry.

As if in reaction, Grant's green eyes darkened. "God, I've missed you." His voice sounded low and rough.

A memory flashed through her mind -- the last time she'd kissed him a decade ago, just before she'd reported to Arcane Corps Basic. She remembered the warm strength of his hands, the feel of his body, tall and strong against hers, the warm heat of his mouth, tasting of mint and frustrated passion. "Of all the things I gave up for the Arcane Corps, I've regretted losing you the most." The admission sounded so naked, it sent a spike of anxiety through her.

"What makes you think you lost me? Margay, *I'm still here.*" Heat flared in his eyes, sharpened his features with need. "And now you are too."

Margay stared up at him, her body going heavy and warm, as if she'd plunged into heated honey. She ached to make love to him again. Ached for the strength, the peace, the raw erotic *delight* of being loved by Grant Sawyer. The one man who could make her forget Ukraine and Afghanistan and Iraq. Forget the things she'd done, the people she'd killed. The mistakes she'd made. Even the devastating moment she'd lost everything.

Including herself.

But you can't. You're not the woman you were ten years ago, and you can't afford the emotional chaos that comes with relationships. Not until you and Raz integrate enough to be safe.

The cat made a low, rumbling sound and flashed her an image -- the memory of Grant when he'd been working to talk her down. There'd been an expression of such worry and love in his eyes, it made her heart ache.

Then a new image appeared: Austin, the last time they'd made love. He'd said all the right things -- that he'd loved her, that they were good together, that they were a fabulous team. Yet his Feral gold eyes had looked so cold she'd known he was lying, despite the lack of deception in his scent. But then, he hadn't smelled of love either, no matter what that glib mouth said.

Grant smelled of love. And some worry, but mostly love. A hot little zing darted through her.

Mmmrooooolf, Raz rumbled in her head. She strongly suspected that was tiger for, "*Jump him while you've got the chance.*" As far as Raz was concerned, they were always in heat.

It's not that simple. "Fact is, I'm going to be a danger to everyone I love until I can control Raz better. Taking a public-facing job under these circumstances is irresponsible. I'm going to have to tell Mama that I quit and go find some kind of remote work."

Huffff. How the cat managed to put that much disgust into such a short sound, Margay didn't know.

Grant apparently agreed, because he frowned. "Margay, shutting yourself off from everyone you care about is not going to help the control problem. Look, you learned to handle combat by *being in combat*, right?"

"I went through a lot of training, but basically… yeah," she admitted. "The Corps did live fire drills with us, but we all knew nobody was actively *trying* to kill us. Nothing can train you for going up against people who want you dead… except combat."

"Same with cops. You can practice at the range all you want, but until you experience a line-of-duty adrenaline dump, you can't guarantee you'll be able to hit the broad side of a barn when the real shooting starts." He wrapped his arms around her and pulled her closer. "If you want to learn how to manage strong emotions, isolating yourself is counterproductive." His voice dropped as his warm gaze meant hers. "Not to mention lonely as hell."

The look in his eyes gave her the courage to say what she was thinking. "God, I'm tired of being lonely. Being alone."

Need heated those green eyes, and he smiled. "Me too." Slowly, giving her plenty of time to pull away if she changed her mind, he bent his head and kissed her. His lips felt like sun-warmed satin as they brushed hers, his tongue slipping out to trace the seam between her lips. At the same time, the circle of his arms loosened, as if to give her the opportunity to step away if this wasn't what she wanted.

Margay had no desire to step away. She *craved* him. Craved him like a drug because she was tired and frustrated and sad. Wanted to forget. Just for a while. She ached to just get away from all this pain.

So she kissed him back with all her starving passion, all the need and loneliness she'd felt for so long. Her tongue swept into his mouth, tasting him. Groaning at the heat and pressure of his body. Familiar, and yet so different from the lean boy she remembered. She could think of no better place to go than into Grant's muscled arms. But… Duty was duty, and that included his. "Do we… do we have time? I mean, how long do you get for lunch?"

"I've been working for fucking sixteen hours straight, and I'm not even halfway through my second shift. I'm taking a long lunch." His lips curved wickedly. "It's not a lie -- I fully intend to do plenty of eating."

Margay laughed and he kissed her again, hot and fierce and delicious. He tasted of her mother's magic-infused roast -- and that indefinable something she associated with Grant. His tongue swirled into her open mouth in slow, seductive licks, and she suckled it, loving the taste of him. His hands glided down her body, tracing the rise of her hip, the curve of her waist. Warm. Strong. Tempting.

God, she'd been so fucking lonely. Even with Austin and all the kinky shit they'd done, there'd always been a barrier between them.

Nothing at all stood between her and Grant.

His body felt so good against hers, hard and strong despite the thick padding of his Kevlar vest. She ached to get him out of that blue uniform, see what ten years had done to his beautiful body. *In case I don't get another chance*.

Sheer need drove her to flatten herself against him as she deepened the kiss, tongue licking hungrily at his. He reacted in kind, his twining and dancing with hers. Inhaling the taste of him, she groaned as heat built in her blood. Her nipples tightened, and a sweet, lush pressure built in her pussy.

Beneath the bottom edge of his vest -- beneath the plastic and gear of his duty belt -- he was hard and thick and long against her belly. Margay gasped in need and pulled away to stare into his handsome, hungry face. "Come to bed." The words shot out of her mouth without stopping off at her brain, but she found she didn't care.

Not when sheer lust tightened his face. "Yeah." The word sounded ragged with need. She grabbed his hand and towed him out of the kitchen and down the hall toward her bedroom, Raz rumbling in happy anticipation the whole way. Tigers didn't purr, but she hadn't gotten the memo.

As they walked in, Margay suddenly realized she hadn't bothered to change the decor since high school. There was the maple queen-size bed, draped in an Autumn gold comforter next to a matching nightstand.

They'd made love on that bed. *Maybe that's why I never redecorated.*

But there was also a 2008 Iron Man poster and towering bookshelves lining three walls, stuffed with science fiction paperbacks, manga and graphic novels. "Damn, I was such a little nerd," she murmured. "I really should redecorate."

"I'd say you made plenty of changes," Grant said, an odd note in his voice. He walked over to the shadow box hanging over the nightstand. Her mother had created it to showcase her service ribbons and neat row of medals: the Silver Star she'd won for beating off the Afghan girls' school attack, the Arcane Corps' Bronze Lion, the Corps' Pentagram for Gallantry. Margay joined him as he brushed a finger over the glass above the Purple Heart. "Which of them is for… what happened with Raz?"

"None of them. I won't be getting a medal for that." *You don't get medals for anything top secret.*

He turned to her, frowning. "Why?"

She shook her head, and grabbed the hem of her Spoon T-shirt and pulled it off in one tug. Her braids pulled upward, then rained around her shoulders again as she dropped the shirt on the floor.

It was a damned good way to change the subject. His eyes widened and went directly to the red lace bra that veiled the curve of her breasts. "That's, uh… A nice bra." He sounded a little hoarse.

It made her smile. "I've been trying to make myself feel a little more me."

"You always did have good taste…" A smile flashed across his face. "In every sense of the word." Grant reached out, almost hesitantly, to cradle her breasts in the soft crimson lace, lifting them, an expression on his face that looked like reverence. It reminded her of their very first time as a pair of high school virgins. They both looked down, admiring the contrast of soft, rich brown skin, red lace -- and his hands, so much paler, long-fingered and strong.

He bent and kissed the top slope of each mound, his lips warm and tender on her skin. She shuddered at feeling his mouth on her again. *At last.*

Finding the bra's front closure, he popped it open, pulling the straps down her arms, watching the fabric fall away. Moving slowly, he cradled her bare breasts. There was nothing rough about the way he touched her, nothing careless. The contrast with Austin…

Okay, that's the last time I'm thinking about that motherfucker. Not when Grant stood so close, green eyes lifting to her face. There was desire in his scent, but beneath that lay something deeper, fiercer. Something she'd missed so much.

She was breathing harder now, each breath rich with his scent. The last time they'd been this close, she hadn't had a tiger spirit's nose to draw upon. Now the lush scent of Grant's desire made her feel drugged.

Margay found the buttons of his uniform shirt, began slipping them free one by one. She had to pause to unplug the handset hooked to the epaulet of his dark blue shirt before she peeled it off. Next, she got rid of his duty belt, heavy with his equipment, then the Kevlar vest, leaving him in a white T-shirt, a little damp with sweat. The rich scent of him made her hunger rise even higher. Raz rumbled a soft crooning sound, reacting to her need.

"My turn." Grant slid the zipper down on her black chinos and slid a hand inside her waistband, then down her red lace panties. Eyes locked on hers, a faint smile on his face, he worked a forefinger between her plump vaginal lips. Found her already wet, already ready. His eyes hooded, he made a soft crooning sound of his own and pushed deeper into her slick and eager heat. Found her opening and slid inside. Margay gasped at the hot pleasure of his slow, pumping strokes. "You feel like hot cream," he whispered. "All tight and ready."

She cupped his thick width through the tough polyester pants. "You... feel pretty damn good yourself." The vest had trapped his scent, and now it rolled from him, rich with sensual pheromones her tiger senses could detect. "But you're still wearing too damn many clothes." Releasing him, she grabbed the hem of the tee and pulled it up and over his head.

Taking a step back, she stared hungrily at him, aware he was eyeing her in return. The lean boy's body he'd had in high school had given way to a man's sculpted muscle and corded power. Nobody would ask if he lifted weights -- it was nakedly obvious he did, between the width of his shoulders, the flat ripples of abdominals, the narrow hips.

Suddenly ferociously impatient, she stepped in again to unfasten his pants and drag them down, only to run into his shoes. She growled a little in frustration, echoed by Raz's deeper grumble. Grant laughed and pulled away to drop down on the bed to take his shoes off.

When he leaned back on the bed, she dragged his pants the rest of the way off, leaving him wearing only a pair of boxers that outlined the thick bulk of his cock. The boxers had to go, as well.

Margay toed off her own shoes and stripped off her black chinos and red panties, leaving them where they lay on the polished wood floor. Looking up, she found Grant watching her, hunger stark on his face, muscular legs braced wide.

God, that cock -- so hard it curved, thick over furry, full balls. Looking at him, remembering the way it had felt when they'd made love a decade ago, raw lust rolled over Margay, hot and ferocious.

She licked her lips and rasped, "My memory didn't do you justice." Margay dropped to her knees and bent forward, about to suck him right into her mouth. She'd always loved giving Grant blowjobs...

"Nope," he said, rising from the bed to pull her to her feet. "If anybody's *anything* is getting sucked..."

"Hey, no fair!"

She tried to cling to his cock, but Grant sat down on the bed and lay back, straight-arming her body over him, then positioning her so her breasts dangled over his mouth. She could feel his breath on her nipples as he purred, "Gimme a minute and you'll find out how fair I can be..."

Opening his mouth wide over one peaked nipple, he sucked in as much of her dangling breast as he could, pulling in sweet tugs that sent pleasure swirling through her. She gasped and braced herself, and he freed one hand to cup her as he scraped his teeth slowly over the soft flesh.

Margay threw her head back, gasping as she braced her elbows on the bed, supporting herself, loving the way he teased her. She tangled her hands in his short, silken curls, letting the pleasure wash away the pain and shame of the morning, of her loss of control. *He's always known what I need better than I do.*

Feeling a little crazed, she braced her knees on the bed, sliding them down until her pussy just brushed the shaft of his cock. Repositioned her knees so she could roll her hips over the rock-hard jut, pressing just close enough to brush her curls over its soft, taut skin.

"You always know just how to drive me crazy," he gasped around her nipple.

As he closed his lips around it for a long, drawing suck, she managed, "Same to... to you. *Ahhh!*" Unable to resist the temptation, she angled her hips lower, teasing his cock more firmly with her pussy. Letting him feel how wet she was. How much she needed him -- had *always* needed him, whether he believed it or not.

She braced on one hand, reaching down to grip his cock, feeling the thickness fill her hand. Giving him long, slow pulls as his busy mouth did exquisite things to first one nipple, then the other.

"Okay. My turn." She pulled away. Before he could drag her back, she shifted off him and pivoted to angle his cock up. Bending, she filled her mouth with its velvet head and her free hand with his balls.

"Jesus!" Grant gasped and arched against her, and she grinned in satisfaction.

Margay pulled off him and started licking up and down his length, getting him good and wet. When she was satisfied, she wrapped her hand around the base of his cock and started sucking the rest of him as far down as she could. Though she'd deep-throated Austin, that wasn't an option with Grant. He was too damn big. *I always did love a challenge…*

She took him deep, deeper, until involuntary tears stung her eyes. Pulled off him, loving the slide of his tight, satin skin over her tongue, the intimate musk of him filling her nose. *Eau de Grant…*

God, so good… So perfect…

He started to wrap his hand into her braids, only to snatch his hand back. Somebody must have told him that wasn't something he should be doing. "We need to slow this down or we're gonna be done way too quick…" he managed, his voice rasping. "I've wanted you way too long to hold off if you keep doing that."

Margay met his gaze, breathing hard, her pussy so wet and swollen that she ached. "All right," she panted, and released him.

Grant rolled her over on her back, then rose over her. Before he could do whatever he had in mind, she caught his handsome face in both hands. "God, I missed you. There were times I thought I'd die from it…"

Green eyes flared wide. He bent his head, taking her mouth in a slow, hot kiss, pressing into her as he braced on powerful arms, kissing her as if she were his last breath. His long legs tangled with hers, his cock hard, still wet with her saliva. She loved that she'd claimed him like that.

He felt so damn good. Even better than the boy she'd adored in those innocent days before she'd bought an E-ticket ride to hell. He kissed along the line of her jaw, nibbling, hungry kisses, and she wrapped both arms around him, loving the feel of his broad back, muscle rolling under her hands.

She stroked the length of his torso, exploring the rippling contours, investigating the hair on his chest, finding tight, tiny male nipples to stroke and pinch.

Grant growled softly and went for the curve of her throat. Enjoying the scrape of his teeth on her skin, she bent her head to run her tongue over his muscular shoulder. Drinking in the taste of salt and male and that delicious Grant smell she'd longed for in her lonely bunk.

She twisted, lifting him and rolling him over so she could straddle him. He looked up at her, startled eyes flaring wide.

She froze, realizing she hadn't had that kind of strength when she'd been with him last. Her muscles tensed. Men did not like her showing how strong Raz made her…

A broad grin spread across his face. "Guess everything they say about Ferals is true."

His gaze slid down her body, paused on the tight brown nipples. His fingers closed on one with exquisite gentleness, tugging, rolling it between thumb and forefinger.

Grant sat up with stomach muscles alone. Margay leaned back as he fastened his mouth around one nipple for a fierce, drawing suck. The sweet, stabbing pleasure made her fling back her head so hard, she felt her braids lash her calves.

"God, you taste soooo good," he rumbled, his voice even deeper and rougher than it normally was, with that low drawl he had.

Supporting her in those powerful arms, he suckled. Margay let her eyes drift closed. And saw Raz, her ears pricked forward and her eyes wide and round. The tiger panted in excitement. *I'm right there with you, sister.*

The radio crackled in the background as she straddled him, acutely aware of the bulk of his cock beneath her, pressing between the folds of her wet cunt. Slowly, deliberately, she rose up on her knees so she could reach down between her legs to grip his cock.

She angled it so she could grind along the length of it without pressing it painfully into his pelvis and belly. Stroked and caressed the thick shaft, the furry balls, enjoying the sensation as she rode against him, letting his hardness tease her clit.

Christ, I'm wet. Austin had never made her this hot, this ready. Just being with Grant lit up every hungry nerve she had.

"You're driving me crazy with that," he panted.

She grinned. "Good."

His voice dropped to a growl. "I'll show you good." He caught her around the waist, picked her up and rolled her to her back on the bed, then came down on top of her again.

"Sixty-nine!" she demanded as he started to move down her body.

"Not this time," he growled, hoarse and determined. "I need all the self-control I can get. I just wish we had time for something more."

"There's always next time," she rasped.

He looked up from between her legs as he settled himself, dark hair in his eyes. There was something vulnerable in his gaze. "There'll *be* a next time?"

"Yeah," she panted. "You're the only way I'm going to get through this. I need you so goddamn bad. Always have…" *But you had to go and…*

She snapped her teeth closed. *Not bringing up Brandy. Especially not now.*

Grant scooped up her legs and folded them double against her chest. He looked down between them, his eyes hungry and naked with need. With a low rumble, he lowered his head and began to lick. Grant knew just where to circle and play, just how to tease. Each tongue flick and suckle inflicted thundering jolts of pleasure that had her arching her back and grabbing his head with both hands.

Christ, so good.

Unlike Austin, he didn't eat her like he was in a hurry for his own pleasure. He lapped her clit slowly, slooowly, then pulled back to swirl his tongue up and down between her pussy lips. Grant took his time, stoking her gathering climax lick by lick. Tightening his lips, he suckled, at just the right angle to maximize the razor-blade delight.

Margay wrapped her legs around his shoulders and hooked her ankles together, unable to resist the need to grind against him, intensifying the sensation of that decadent tongue.

Panting, she strained, hunching hard to the sound of Raz's thrumming rumble and the crackle of the radio. The orgasm went off like a MEED, a burst of pulsing heat that made her see sparks of magic explode behind closed lids.

She yowled, and so did Raz, the pleasure throwing her high, making the world swim around her…

Then Grant was out from between her legs… Only to freeze, looking down at her, wide eyed with dismay. "Shit. Tell me you've got condoms!"

"Uh…" She stared back, nonplused, then reached out and fumbled in a drawer. And yeah, there was a sleeve of them. She tore one off, ripped the package open, slid it over that thick, delicious shaft.

Growling -- sounding a whole lot like Raz -- he positioned himself over her. Finally -- *finally*! -- that tempting cock found the slick, swollen opening of her pussy. And thrust inside. Slowly, the fight for control stark on his face, as if she were a virgin.

But her hunger -- and Raz's -- blazed in her blood, and she grabbed his ass in both hands and began to roll, grinding, surging against him.

He grunted, sending her a startled glance.

Shit! Margay jerked her hands away, "Did I scratch you?" She shot a look at her hands. *No claws, thank God.*

"No, he rasped. "I like it when you hold me like that."

So she relaxed again as he went back to thrusting, fucking her in plunging strokes, no longer holding back, as if finally realizing she hadn't been a virginal teenager in a decade. Pleasure surged through her, and she let her head fall back, keening, begging.

Back with him at last.

* * *

Grant fought to hold on. Margay felt so incredibly tight and slick, and it had been too damn long. Too goddamn long since making love had made his soul quake.

Her tight inner muscles worked along his length, milking his starving cock. Until the sheer silky pleasure of it was too much for him, and he came with a strangled shout.

He heard her deep, gathering rumble, recognized the building sound, and gasped, "*Don't roar, Margay*!"

Her teeth clamped shut as she stiffened, golden

eyes rolling back as raw pleasure twisted her lovely face.

They came, bodies convulsing, heaving against each other, riding out an even stronger climax. Until they collapsed together in a sweating, limp heap.

"Damn it, that didn't take long enough," Grant panted.

"Worked for me." Margay grinned up at him, white teeth flashing in a puckish grin he knew so well.

Which, of course, was when his cell rang.

"Oh, for fuck's sake! Really?" she grumbled.

"We were lucky to get what we did." Grant sighed, rolling reluctantly to his feet to fish the phone out of his pants.

The display read CSI. "Chief Grant Sawyer. How may I help you?"

"Crime Scene Investigator Barry Raines. What have you got, chief?"

Aaaand, there went the last of the afterglow, blown out like a match by that ugly reminder. "We had what looks like a MEED. Went off in the middle of the lunch rush at Mama's Spoon."

Raines lost his bored indifference. "Holy Jesus! Any injuries?"

"No, nothing like that. We suspect it was more an attempt to drive a veteran over the edge. A fireworks detonation that sounded like a mass shooter."

"What makes you so sure it's a MEED?" The CSI was sounding downright dubious now.

"Two people with a lot more magic than me. I need you to collect all the fireworks debris and the cardboard box they came in. Then use a black light to check for sigils in ultraviolet paint. We have reason to believe there will be some. Also, there may be some potion residue. If you can collect that, I want to send it to the SLED Arcane lab for analysis."

"Okay. I'll be there in thirty."

Grant winced a little. That would barely give him enough time to get showered and cleaned up. He really didn't want to meet the investigators smelling like sex. "Thanks, Raines. See you then."

He hung up as Margay stepped over to him and draped her arms around his neck, a wicked smile on her lips as she asked, "Want to share a shower?"

"Love to, but we'd still be at it when CSI rolled up downstairs and wondered where the hell I was."

Margay stretched lazily against him, all smooth, dark skin and lush seduction. "Good point." She licked her lips, lids dipping over golden eyes. "We'll have to try it later."

Oh, God, I hope so, Grant thought. And prayed she wouldn't change her mind.

Because he needed her for a lot more than sex.

Chapter Five

Margay lay on her bed, listening to the shower run. Her body felt loose and boneless, almost glowing in the aftermath of fabulous sex. For the first time in months, she felt like herself. Felt as if she wasn't broken. Wasn't a grenade with a pulled pin, waiting for the boom.

It wasn't just the sex, either. It was the way Grant looked at her. As if she was someone he admired. Someone he loved. Austin had never made her feel anything like this.

Grant walked out of her en suite bath, drying his hair with a towel. He paused in the doorway, staring at her, and she stared right back. Runnels of water ran down that amazing body, and unable to resist, she rolled out of bed. Taking the towel from him, she started drying his back, lingering on his muscular ass, the length of his long legs, pausing here and there to run her nails over sensitive spots.

He grinned over his shoulder at her. "Keep that up, I'm gonna be late to work."

"Just making sure you don't get your pants wet," she purred, rising to toss the towel into the hamper.

Grant laughed and headed for the pile of his clothing and gear. Leaning on the maple dresser, Margay watched him dress in unabashed lust.

He slanted a look at her. "Would you put on a robe or something? I don't want to have to go downstairs to talk to CSI with a massive hard-on."

"And God knows, that thing is hard to miss." Laughing, she headed for the closet and pulled on a red satin robe. *I need a shower too,* she decided, getting a whiff of herself as she tied the robe closed.

When she looked around, he was buckling on his duty belt and eyeing her. "How much sleep did you get last night?"

"More than you, even with the nightmare."

"Then why don't you take a nap for both of us? If I know my mom, she'll probably talk yours into a shopping expedition on top of lunch. You can take a hot shower and drink one of your mother's teas." He grimaced. "Take it from me, life's a lot less traumatic when you're not sleep-deprived. And I doubt a lack of sleep makes Raz any easier to contain."

"Good point." She sighed and headed for the shower.

But as she passed, he reached out to catch the lapel of her robe, gently tugging her closer. She went for the kiss at the same time he did, and they leaned body to body, mouths open and hungry, tongues stroking and swirling.

Until the radio crackled. "Hey, Chief," Roger said. "I see the CSI van coming up the street."

Grant sighed and triggered his handset. "10-4. On my way down." Pulling reluctantly away, he gave her a smile. "See you later."

"Tonight?" she asked. "Let me know what you find out." She stroked a quick hand over his cheek as he turned to head for the door.

Margay licked her lips, tasting toothpaste. He must've made use of one of the wrapped toothbrushes she socked away whenever she went to the dentist. He used to do that when they were in high school.

She locked up behind him, then padded to the shower.

* * *

While she waited for the men to change out of

their Spook Suits, Anastasia went to work on the second phase of the plan.

The members of the team had been provided with false identities and assorted email addresses, along with accompanying legends -- false backgrounds that would make them appear to be American citizens if anyone did a background check. GRU had provided forged documents for Austin as well, though the aliases would be shakier than theirs. If the police managed to collect any careless fingerprints, he'd pop on the government database from his service in the Arcane Corps. But there wasn't much to do about that except make sure he didn't *get* careless.

Now she used one of her own false email addresses to send the video she and Karl had shot to the local television stations. The accompanying email was designed to catch the attention of any reporter or news producer that received it.

"I just wanted to make you aware of the terrifying experience I had today," she'd written. "I was at lunch at Mama's Spoon, an Ashburg restaurant, when one of their Feral employees went crazy and manifested a magical tiger in the middle of lunch. It scared everybody to death. I thought it was going to eat us -- it roared and acted like it was going to attack any minute. We had to evacuate the restaurant.

"I think it's irresponsible for the restaurant to have one of those Ferals working there. Everybody knows those people are demon possessed. That woman could go crazy again, and customers might not get off so lucky the next time."

Smiling faintly, Anastasia hit the *send* button.

Yeah, she'd hoped for a little more bloodshed, but the video gave them enough to work with. Especially once she finished singing to the right people.

It was ridiculously easy to panic norms if you knew what you were doing.

* * *

Grant opened the downstairs door and stepped out to find Roger Porter leaning against the wall, looking just a little bit knowing.

"Well, you look in a much better mood than you did when you went up the stairs," the older cop drawled.

"I was interviewing the witnesses." Oh, God, were his cheeks getting hot?

Porter blinked in pretended innocence. "Is that what the kids are calling it these days?"

Grant gave his subordinate his best icy glower, which had been working on patrol cops since he'd made detective. It bounced right off Roger, who'd been friends with Margay's dad.

That was the thing about becoming chief in a department where everyone knew everyone. Nobody could keep their nose in their own business.

Before he could think of a suitably stinging retort, the white Crime Scene Unit van pulled in behind their SUVs. Two techs in olive green coveralls got out and headed for them.

The man -- his I.D. plate read "Lt. B. Raines, Crime Scene Investigations" -- was a tall, skinny man not far from retirement, with a bony face and the cynical gaze of someone who had seen virtually every revolting thing one human could do to another.

His assistant was a willowy black woman who wore her hair in a tight cap of dark curls. Her plate read "Katila Simmons." In marked contrast to her boss, her eyes looked bright and interested, and Grant wondered how long it would take her job to rub the shine off all that obvious idealism.

He felt old as hell just looking at her.

"So what have we got?" Raines asked, pulling out a pen and a narrow paper notebook.

"What appears to be a bakery box full of fireworks was planted behind a counter in the restaurant. It went off, making virtually everyone in the room think they had an active shooter."

The investigator grunted as he started scribbling notes.

"So far no one saw it brought in, but we're going to canvas the witnesses to double-check."

Raines looked up. "Any of them still here?"

"No, we had to evacuate. But I have a list of who was here, and I know a lot of them. Don't expect to have much trouble running them down."

The investigator grunted. "Should have corralled them before they left."

"At the time," Grant said patiently, "We had a Feral tiger manifestation to deal with. I was just trying to get everyone out of the restaurant."

"And I was on the way to the jail with a prisoner," Roger put in, "So he was shorthanded."

Raines looked up, frowning. "Did you say you had a Feral tiger? How the fuck did that happen?"

Grant shrugged. "The owner's daughter is an Arcane Corps vet. She was in the back when the fireworks went off, and she manifested her cat, thinking they were under attack."

Raines' frown deepened. "I assume you charged her under the Bright Act. Given she manifested in public…"

Grant felt the muscles tighten in his shoulders, though he kept his anger off his face. "I'm not planning to charge her at this time. From what I gather, it sounded like World War III in the dining room, and her mother screamed. The Bright Act has an exception for manifesting when the public is in danger."

The investigator's eyes narrowed in disapproval. "Sounds like the public was in more danger from her than a box of firecrackers. I mean, considering you had to evacuate…"

"She didn't hurt anyone, so an arrest wasn't warranted." Not in the mood for an argument on the subject, Grant said, "I'd like you to look for a detonator, because if someone had carried in a box of lit fireworks, they'd gone off before he got in the door."

"Staff could have just been distracted."

"I'd still like you to use a black light to check the box remains for sigils written in ultraviolet paint. I strongly suspect an Arcanist was involved, because the Feral and her mother told me they detected the smell of magic. They think the reason nobody saw anyone bring the box in was that an invisibility spell was written on the box."

Raines grunted. "Simplest explanation is usually the best. And if it was the middle of the lunch rush…"

"Yes, but the owner said she kicked something behind the counter. When she looked down, there was nothing there. Her daughter said the Caliphate often cast invisibility spells on MEEDs, which would explain why nobody saw the box."

The investigator looked up from his notes again, his expression more than a little suspicious. "If it was a MEED, why is there still a building?"

"We don't think it was that kind of MEED."

"Who's we?" His gaze fell on the sign, then widened. "Mama's Spoon? Wasn't that place on *Magical Kitchens*? The owner's an Alchemist, right?

Jasmine something…"

"Jocelyn," Grant corrected. "Jocelyn Whitfield."

"Yeah, that's her. Okay, got it. We'll get this stuff collected. You taking it to SLED?" SLED was the South Carolina Law Enforcement Division, which was the state's answer to the FBI. Its crime lab handled DNA, ballistics, and magical evidence processing that county sheriff's offices and police departments couldn't do themselves.

Grant nodded. "I'll send Officer Porter to Columbia with it in the morning."

"Good idea," Raines said. "By the time we finish processing the scene, there won't be time to drive it to SLED before the lab closes." He turned to his assistant. "Let's unload the gear and get started. I'd like to have this finished by five."

Grant left them to it and took Porter aside. "I've got a list of lunch customers from Jocelyn. There are about thirty names, including the restaurant staff. I've emailed you fifteen of the names. You can pull the addresses off the system. Ask them what they saw -- record the interviews if possible. Maybe we'll get lucky."

Roger looked a little dubious. "If this clown really was invisible, nobody saw shit."

"Maybe. Or we could have a smart ass teenager playing a prank on the worst possible people. We need to eliminate horses before we start hunting zebras."

Porter snorted. "Yeah, the sound of hoof beats can come from a lot of things." He grimaced. "Including demons."

"Don't even joke."

* * *

Grant started with visits to the restaurant staff

who'd been on duty -- Brenda Hollings, the other waitress, and Jocelyn's assistant alchemist cooks Shana Price and Joe Jeffries.

Price and Jeffries hadn't seen anyone come in with a box -- no surprise, considering the two had been in the kitchen helping with meal prep. Both asked how Margay and Jocelyn were doing, sounding genuinely concerned. Neither could think of anyone who'd have a reason to want to hurt the women, and they seemed indignant about the idea anyone would.

That opinion was echoed by Brenda Hollings, a thirty-five-year-old brunette who'd waitressed at the restaurant for ten years. She invited him into her neat little ranch, which was decorated in Early American Mother. Every surface in the house held a piece of kid artwork, including the crayon scribbles on the walls.

"As if Margay hasn't suffered enough," she growled. She was a small woman, with the soft build and maternal air of a born caretaker.

When he asked if the restaurant had any trouble with humanists, Brenda snorted. "A couple of assholes left nasty Yelp reviews accusing the boss of using her 'satanic' powers on the customers. The satanic allegation worried me some -- I was afraid we'd get swarmed by Humanist trolls. But I told some of the regulars, and they mobilized the rest of our customers to leave so many five-star reviews, it canceled the assholes out."

He wasn't surprised. Jocelyn tended to inspire that kind of loyalty in people. She was always the first to organize a GoFundMe for any family who'd suffered a fire, serious medical diagnosis, or a sudden death. Everybody knew if you needed help, the Whitfield family would lead the charge.

Then there was the food. As one Yelp reviewer

had put it, *"The Spoon's fried chicken is the next best thing to a religious experience."*

"You know the name of these two Humanist jerks?"

"Yeah, and so do you," Brenda told him. "One of them was Jimmy Miller. I heard him brag about it over at Six Shooters a couple of days after the review went up."

One of my officers is running off at the mouth. In a bar. Grant ground his teeth. "When did he do this?"

She shrugged. "It was before you were hired. Maybe a year and a half ago. But I don't think Jimmy would be dumb enough to plant that box."

I don't know about that. Jimmy's pretty dumb. Grant had realized the young cop was a Humanist after the idiot made a nasty joke about beating Talents. Grant had hauled him into his office and told him that shit wasn't acceptable.

The officer had acted all wounded and claimed he'd only been joking, then that he hadn't meant it, then that he was entitled to his opinion. Which was three different explanations for the same thing, suggesting it was all bullshit.

"Yes, you are entitled to your opinion," Grant had told him coldly. "What you aren't entitled to do is let your opinion influence your actions while you're in that uniform. I'd better not find out you abused your badge, because I will fire you, uncle or no uncle. So do *not* give me a reason."

Of course, Jimmy was supposedly out of town, and in any case, he had all the magic of a paperweight. Whoever had planted that box was a Talent.

He said his goodbyes to Brenda and went off to the next witness on his list.

* * *

Grant walked into Shear Excellence to find Elaine Bates at work on an elderly lady whose neat cap of wet hair was dyed a vivid peacock blue. "Hello, ladies," he began, as he pulled out his cell. "Elaine, I've got some questions about what you saw at the Spoon today. I'm trying to find out who's responsible."

"And I hope you kick his butt when you do," Elaine growled. "Damn kids."

Her customer twisted around, and a broad grin lit her wrinkled face. "Grant! There you are. We were just talking about that mess at the Spoon."

Which was when he recognized her. "Mrs. Jones! Hi. Didn't recognize you with that hair."

Her smile turned puckish. "One of my students called me a blue-haired old lady, so I decided to play to the stereotype."

He blinked -- she had to be in her seventies. "Are you still teaching fourth grade?"

"Lord, no. I retired years ago. I tutor kids in English now." She grimaced. "God knows they need it. None of them has the least idea where to put a period, never mind commas."

Grant grinned, remembering how Mrs. Jones's classroom library had gotten him and Margay hooked on science fiction. He held up his cell. "Do y'all mind if I record this?" he asked. "I'm trying to track down whoever planted those firecrackers."

"No, go right ahead," Mrs. Jones said, waving a wrinkled hand.

Brenda agreed, and Grant turned on his phone's recording app and identified himself and both women for the record. "How are y'all doing?" he asked. "I saw you at the Spoon."

"Oh, I'm fine," the stylist said, and shook her head. "I just felt so sorry for Jocelyn and Margay. Are they both okay? I'll bet Margay feels awful."

"Jocelyn's fine. Margay's pretty shaken."

"I'm not surprised -- when that thing first went off, I thought we were under fire," Mrs. Jones put in. "My Tom would have had a flashback too." She shook her head. "Every Fourth of July, he thought he was back in Vietnam. What a heaping helping of *hell* that was."

"Did either of you see how the fireworks got into the restaurant?"

"That's the weird thing," the old woman said. "I was sitting in the booth across from the Square station, and I had a good view behind that counter. When Nancy called Jocelyn to the phone, I glanced over. There was absolutely *nothing* there. When the first pop went off, it looked like the light from the fireworks appeared in midair."

Sounded like Margay and her mother were right -- there was a spell involved. "Then what happened?"

"Jocelyn and Nancy leaped away -- I think Jocelyn got burned -- and they both tripped and went down. I jumped up and saw a box just... *appear* out of nowhere. A minute later, the fireworks blew it apart. Pieces everywhere."

Elaine frowned. "That sounds like magic."

Mrs. Jones nodded. "That was my thought."

Elaine had nothing to add, since she'd been seated near the front of the dining room and had no view behind the counter. Neither of them had seen anyone walk in with a box.

His mind chewing over the implications, Grant said his goodbyes, put his phone away, and walked out.

Anastasia Yakovna sat behind the wheel of the battered Honda Prelude she'd bought for this job, watching as the cop got in his SUV and drove off. *He could be a problem.* Sawyer might become suspicious if the stylist's new version of events didn't jibe with whatever she'd told him a few minutes ago.

Then again, everyone knew witnesses lied -- especially to the police.

Judging that the coast was clear, Anastasia slid from her car and strolled into Shear Excellence.

It was a small salon, with only two stations, a sink for washing hair, and an artificial Christmas tree hung with tiny toy combs, hair dryers and pairs of scissors.

"I remember when those two were kids," an old lady was saying to the stylist. Her hair, oddly, was dyed a bright peacock blue that matched her polyester slacks. She wore a protective poncho covered with reindeer and sleds. "One time there was this little bully who tried to pick on Margay. Grant slammed his head into a water fountain. Actually put a dent in it, too. Grant got suspended, of course, but that little jerk never said another word to Margay."

Well, isn't that interesting, Anastasia thought. *The chief has a conflict of interest. That is something we can use.*

She'd have to ask Austin about it. If Margay still had a thing for the police chief, Austin would know. The man was obsessed with that woman.

The stylist finally noticed Anastasia and said, "Oh, hello. Have a seat, I'll be with you in a few."

"Sorry I'm late," Anastasia said. She'd had to wait ten minutes for the chief to leave.

"Oh, it's no problem," the woman said. "I'm

running late myself."

"Weren't y'all at that restaurant today?" Anastasia asked as she headed for a chair, speaking in a slow southern drawl she'd worked hard to perfect. "The food was delicious, but that tiger scared the life out of me."

"Oh, you had nothing to worry about," the stylist said, waving a hand. "Margay Whitfield would never hurt a soul. She's a war hero -- she's just going through a bad patch."

"I'd like to find the jerk who planted those firecrackers and kick his backside," the old woman growled. "As if Margay hadn't been through enough."

Anastasia stared at her, disconcerted. *Little bitch is town hero. This might complicate things.*

Then she shook off the thought. It didn't matter what the women thought now because they wouldn't be thinking it for long. "But if she goes crazy over a prank, she's dangerous!" Anastasia said earnestly.

"Oh, it was no prank," the babushka said. "That was a MEED. The box with the firecrackers was invisible, then it appeared after the fireworks started going off. So that wasn't some kid's idea of a joke. It was an attack."

It was a good thing Anastasia was as experienced as she was, or her astonishment might have shown. "What makes you think that? Wouldn't a MEED have killed everybody?"

"Not if somebody wanted to terrorize people by setting Margay off. The assholes. But Grant will take care of them." She turned to the mirror and patted her short blue hair. Why was a *babushka* getting a teenager's dye job? "The color is perfect. The kids will love it."

I'm running out of time. I need to get this old suka

under control before she runs her mouth to people who matter.

Normally Anastasia would have simply used her voice to put them both gently under, but the *babushka* was getting ready to leave, and she'd seen too much. Anastasia pulled on her power and began to sing "Silent Night," starting off low and soft, barely more than a hum, then increasing the volume until her voice poured over the women, the words of the beautiful old hymn soaring high and sweet, each note ringing with her power.

The two women turned to stare, eyes widening in surprise that rapidly segued into entranced delight.

"You have a lovely voice," the old woman said when she finished, already sounding a little dazed.

Yes, Anastasia thought. *Yes, I do.* And then she started singing the next song, sinking her magic into their minds, opening a way into their memories. Soon they'd believe only what she wanted them to.

And it wouldn't be that Margay Whitfield was an innocent victim.

* * *

Margay walked between the enclosures that housed the Familiars toward the stairs that led out of the bunker on the Charivnyk military base. With every step, her dreaming mind screamed, *No! Go back! They're going to die!*

Czar raced the length of his enclosure, keeping pace with her, making deep moaning roars of distress.

She seemed to be walking in slow motion as she climbed the stairs. For a moment, it seemed she could see herself through the big tiger's eyes -- feel his fear and despair.

No, goddamn it! She yelled at her dreaming self.

Go back, lock it down -- lock the Goddamn building down!

* * *

Margay bolted upright in bed, her heart slamming in her chest, her cheeks wet. Angrily, she knuckled away the tears. *Christ, if I'd just locked the enclosure wing down, none of this would have happened.* Some Russian shithead must have gotten in when she was barely a block away. Too far to save Raz and Czar.

But… How did Czar know? The thought slammed into her consciousness like a runaway train. Why hadn't she seen it before? It was almost like…

Pain detonated in her skull like a lightning strike, so viciously intense she collapsed back on the bed with a cry of agony, echoed by Raz's basso growl.

"Shit shit shit!"

Half blinded by the pain, Margay rolled out of bed and staggered down the hall to the kitchen. Groping for the refrigerator door handle, she jerked it open and grabbed a bottle of PowerUp, unscrewed the cap, and started chugging it down.

Unfortunately, judging by the relentless pulsing throb, even that wasn't going to be good enough to douse the migraine.

She filled a kettle with water and searched the cupboard until she located a jar of her mother's migraine potion. While the water came to a boil, Margay spooned the tea into a mesh brewing ball. When the teapot began to whistle, she dunked the ball into a mug and poured the water over it. Head throbbing viciously, she spooned enough Splenda into the tea to make it drinkable, then carried it to the sectional and sat down to sip. It tasted vile, but she'd guzzle worse to get rid of the pain.

The throbbing soon simmered into a dull pulsing

that gradually faded altogether. Mom always insisted she wasn't good enough to work for a pharmaceutical company, but her tea worked better than most of the migraine potions Margay had tried. And she didn't run the risk of becoming addicted -- in part because it tasted like a dirty gym sock.

Damn, that hurt. What brought that on? She hadn't even been using magic. Margay frowned. She'd had some kind of nightmare -- something about... Czar? But even as she tried to remember, the dream dissolved from her awareness like mist in the sun.

She growled in disgust and took a deeper drink of the cooling tea, watching the tree lights flash. She'd been having this kind of attack for months now. The V.A. neurologist -- also an Arcanist healer -- had told her it was probably an aftereffect of the explosion.

"You're lucky as hell that's *all* that happened to you," Dr. Saban had told her during her last visit. "You could have lost your cat spirit *and* gotten sucked into death with her. That's the kind of stunt that gets you a posthumous medal of honor. I assure you, your mother would rather have you than a folded flag and a chunk of metal on a ribbon."

"Yeah, well, I saved thirty Ukrainian Ferals and every one of their Familiars. If I have to deal with a few headaches, it's a small price to pay."

Now, as the pain subsided, she stood and stepped up beside the Christmas tree, pushing the curtain behind it aside to look out.

Which was when she saw a white van roll up to park diagonally in a space in front of the Spoon.

On its roof was a satellite dish.

She almost dropped the mug. *Oh shit, a news van! I was afraid of that.* Somebody had called the television station. That was all the hell they needed.

Quickly, she pulled out her cell and checked the time. She'd been asleep for only an hour or so. Her mother and Nancy were probably still in Laurelton. She started punching buttons as she whirled and hurried into her bedroom to dress.

Her mother picked up. "Hi, baby."

"Mom…"

"What's wrong?" Sudden alarm rang in her mother's voice.

"News van just pulled up outside the Spoon."

"Oh, Lord."

"I'm gonna go down and talk to them."

"Margay, I'm not sure that's a good idea…"

"I can handle them. I'll call back when I find out what they want. Bye, Mom." She clicked off and turned toward her closet. For a moment she was tempted to put on her Corps uniform -- she was technically in the Reserves. But no, that would be tacky.

Instead, she pulled on jeans and an Arcane Corps sweatshirt, then shoved her feet into her kicks and hustled downstairs.

Even as she descended the steps, she could hear knuckles hitting the door in demanding raps. As she reached for the door, she heard Roger tell the visitor, "The owner's not doing interviews." *Bless him.*

"What's she got to hide?" a male voice demanded. "Because anyone who was on *Magical Kitchens* isn't exactly camera shy."

Margay unlocked the door and pulled it open, almost getting the man's knuckles in the face. She caught his hand and eyed him. "No, my mother *isn't* camera shy," Margay drawled. "And neither am I."

A man she recognized as a local reporter looked down at her, his dark eyes widening. He had a handsome face with rich brown skin and a deep, pleasant baritone. And he was as tall as Austin in his three-piece navy suit, with shoulders that suggested he'd attended college on a football scholarship.

So he looked startled when he tried to pull his hand back and Margay refused to let go, sending a silent *Don't Fuck With Me message*. She gave him a deliberately stony stare, knowing her Feral gold eyes looked even more startling against her brown skin.

The reporter looked taken aback, but he recovered quickly and tried to shift his grip into a handshake. "Nice to meet you. I gather you're Margay Whitfield?"

Margay didn't let go. His eyes narrowed, and he pulled harder, trying to twist out of her grasp. *Yep, definitely football*. She had to tighten her grip.

Point made, she released him with a sunny smile. "And you'd be Darius Palmer with WSAG." *Probably not a good idea to piss off a reporter, but I'm not in the mood, so fuck him*. And her headache was coming back, damn it.

"What brings you to our little town?" Margay looked from him to his videographer, a muscular blonde woman in a jacket with a WSAG-TV logo. She held her camera balanced on her right shoulder, one eye hidden by the viewfinder.

Palmer squared his shoulders and lifted the mic in his free hand. "I'm checking out a video someone sent in today. It seemed to show there was trouble at your restaurant today. A tiger manifested in the dining room of Mama's Spoon. It looked like you were getting ready to attack the diners."

She lifted a brow at him and said dryly, "Yet you came anyway. Brave of you."

He eyed her, his expression equally cool. "I see

you've got crime scene tape up here. Have you been charged under the Bright Act?"

"No, I have not, because I didn't violate the Bright Act. The tape is up because someone set off a magically enhanced explosive device in the middle of my mother's restaurant. And she was standing a foot away when it happened."

His eyes widened and took on a slightly carnivorous glint. "I hope she wasn't hurt." He looked pointedly at the Spoon's plate-glass window. "And the restaurant is, fortunately, still standing."

"It wasn't that kind of MEED. It seems to have been a box full of fireworks."

He looked a bit disappointed and deflated. "A prank, then."

"A prank that sounded like some of the more interesting firefights I was in back in Afghanistan. My mother screamed and I thought we had a mass shooter. I manifested and went to the rescue."

"But judging by the tape one of your diners sent in, you stayed manifested, growling at everyone there. Your mother and the police chief had to talk you down." Palmer looked down at his tablet and thumbed an app on the screen, then turned the device around so she could see it.

Vertical video that appeared to have been shot on a cell phone showed Raz crouching three feet from Mama, glowing, snarling, and generally acting like a cat getting ready to eat someone.

Margay stared, feeling sick. She'd known intellectually it must have been bad, but she hadn't realized just *how* bad.

"The viewer who sent in the video said she was in fear for her life…"

Margay looked up at him, lifting a brow. "She's

got steady hands for someone so terrified."

"Well, considering it looks like you were getting ready to maul your own mother…"

"I didn't hurt my mother -- or anybody else," Margay said through her teeth. "Like many other combat veterans, I find fireworks triggering."

"You suffer from PTSD?" he suggested, his tone syrupy with sympathy even as his expression implied she was crazy as a shithouse rat.

"I'm in treatment," Margay said shortly. "And doing well, as witnessed by the fact I maintained control. Nobody was injured, no thanks to whoever planted the MEED." She almost mentioned the potion they suspected had been packaged with the fireworks, only to realize Grant might not want that information getting out yet. Besides, there was no proof there had been a potion to begin with.

"What makes you think this was a MEED?"

"You'll have to ask the police chief about that."

"Oh, come on, you're a Talent. I understand you people can tell when magic is involved. This sounds more like a prank."

He was beginning to piss her off. "How exactly do you set off a cardboard box full of fireworks without them going off in your hand?"

He studied her over his mic. "That kind of spell would've taken an Arcanist, wouldn't it? How many Arcanists do you have in Ashburg? That should tell you who did it."

"There are no Arcanists in Ashburg. My mother, her two assistant cooks, and I are the only Talents in town."

"Where *is* your mother? I'd like to talk to her."

"She's gone to lunch. Should be back later. If you have any other questions, talk to the police chief."

He gave her a toothy grin. "Yes, I think I'll do that."

As he turned to his videographer, it occurred to her that Grant might not appreciate having the media sicced on him.

Well, hell.

Chapter Six

Brooding, Austin listened as Anastasia and Karl discussed their strategy for the second half of the night. Which apparently involved hanging out in bars while Anastasia bespelled everyone who got close enough to hear her speak.

For once, his own job was going to be much more exciting -- and risky. He felt a hot adrenaline sizzle of anticipation. *This is going to be fun.*

That, or a complete goddamn disaster.

Not for the first time in the past six months, he wondered how much of what he was doing was really his idea.

Hell, when the Bard first recruited him, he'd wondered if he was under one of her vocal spells himself. Why else would he even consider throwing his Arcane Corps career away to become a fucking traitor?

In fact, he strongly suspected Anastasia had used her magic to keep him from killing her when he'd found out she was Russian intelligence.

But once she'd told him about the cool half-million the Russians were offering for his help, he'd started seeing the advantages of the deal.

She'd also had a point about how unjust it was that the Arcane Corps had ignored all his hard work, his skill, his sheer heroism. How they'd passed over him for that last promotion, the one that should have meant a command of his own stateside, rather than training Ukrainian Ferals under the constant threat of Russian artillery.

Meanwhile, they'd given that bitch Margay a Silver Star for some insignificant battle she'd fought during the Afghan evacuation.

Yeah, she'd saved women and girls at that school, but so what? The bitch shouldn't even *have* that tiger -- Raz should have gone to a man. Giving a big predator to Margay just because she ticked the right boxes -- black and female -- was straight-up bullshit.

Somehow Anastasia had sensed how that injustice ate at him. She'd recognized his strength, physically and magically -- and what a deadly team he and Czar really were.

Besides, she fucked like burning vodka: hot, fierce, and intoxicating. She was so damn good he was willing to forget the humiliation of taking orders from a woman half his size.

But then, even Karl took Anastasia's orders, though by all rights, the Bard should be at the bottom of the trio's magical pecking order. Both Austin and Karl had far more power than she did in every sense of the word.

But whenever Anastasia said his name in that purring, guttural accent of hers -- when she wasn't playing American -- Austin wanted to follow her anywhere she led. Do anything to win her respect. Especially something he was dying to do anyway.

Like destroying Margay Whitfield, who'd fucked their Ukrainian plans so thoroughly.

Yeah, tonight was going to be sweeeeet.

* * *

Off duty at last, Grant lay staring up at the ceiling, trying to drift off to sleep despite the memories of Margay's body pressed against his again, all lush curves and eager heat.

He'd thought he'd never taste that lovely mouth again, never feel her rolling against him, the highlights on her skin reminding him of moonlight on satin, impossibly beautiful. Shining in a way paler skin never did.

The thought of being without her -- nothing more than her friend because she'd found another Talent to love -- had filled him with such despair, he'd finally gone looking for a cure for his obsession with her.

In retrospect, he had no idea why he'd ever found Brandy McAllister appealing, despite the pretty face and surface charm.

Margay was *real* in a way his ex would never be. And it had nothing to do with looks. Beautiful as Margay was, it was her brilliance, her talent and her old-fashioned sense of honor that drew him.

Honor he wasn't sure he could claim himself.

His mind slid back to the taste of her mouth, her sweat-slick skin. The feel of her thighs sliding against his. Her nipples stirring the hair on his chest. The taste of her pussy, lush, salty, astringent, flavored with a hint of something inexpressible that must be magic. That taste was even stronger now that they were adults, a reflection of the fact that she and her cat had melded into one being.

His cock rose at the thought of her mouth, the memory of her pussy's slick heat. Lust clawing at him, Grant slid one hand down his naked body and closed on his cock's eager jut.

Something growled -- a deep feline rumble that made ice roll down his spine. He froze.

Raz?

For a moment, his heart leaped. *Margay's here*! He rolled out of bed and grabbed the jeans he'd worn that evening, sliding them up his legs and over his hips, began buttoning and zipping…

She wouldn't just walk into my house without knocking. That stopped him again, and he listened, barely breathing.

Another growl sounded, this one even deeper, more menacing, followed by a hiss.

He'd never heard Raz hiss. Growl, snarl, and roar, sure. But she'd never hissed.

Something's wrong. Is that Raz?

There's an Arcanist involved in this. Maybe an Alchemist. Is there a Feral too?

Shit shit shit. He slipped toward the closet and opened it, revealing the rifle case that held the AR-15 he'd bought after the Faraday Square massacre, when he'd watched that damned polar bear Feral maul a cop to death. He knelt and pulled the rifle out of the case, then dug in a side pouch for one of the magazines he had loaded and ready.

Claws clicked in the hallway.

Shit, that's a full manifestation. Could Margay be under another spell? She would *never* come after him like this unless magic was involved, and neither would Raz. The tiger liked him.

But what if it isn't her? He slid the magazine home and chambered a round.

Unfortunately, the Faraday Square Massacre had demonstrated one or two shots, even with an AR-15, could not puncture a manifestation. That took sustained fire, and there were neighboring houses on either side of his. If he missed, the weapon's high-velocity rounds were far too likely to go right through the walls of the house... *and* the walls of surrounding houses. He didn't dare fire unless he was sure he wouldn't miss. *Should I just stay put?*

But aside from the fact he *really* hated the idea, a manifestation could walk through walls.

Besides, he was damned if he was going to cower.

Carrying the gun, Grant padded to his nightstand and picked up his phone, slid it into the back pocket of his jeans, and headed for the door. Pulled it open.

The tiger crouched at the other end of the darkened hallway in the entrance to the living room, glowing, fully manifested. Her growl rumbled, voice so deep, he could feel it in his breastbone.

He recognized the distinctive stripe pattern, both from yesterday and photos Margay had sent him years ago.

Raz.

Oh, hell. His heart was beating so hard, it thundered in his ears.

"Margay?" He could feel his vision tunneling down, his hearing going metallic and sharp. His mouth tasted of brass -- all signs of an adrenaline dump. "Margay, wake up, honey. It's Grant. You're fine, you're safe. Nobody's going to hurt you."

The tiger roared, a shattering blast of noise that beat his eardrums. Grant jolted back before he could catch himself. His inner prey animal shrieked at him to run, but he knew that was the exact wrong thing to do. It took an effort, but he stayed where he was, inhaling deeply -- *one, two, three, four* -- trying to use tactical breathing to slow his thundering heart and keep his forebrain from going off-line. An adrenaline dump could make you do some seriously stupid shit.

He stared into the cat's face as she crept toward him, looking for Margay. She should be inside the manifestation like she had been at lunch…

There was nothing there. The cat was translucent, and he could see through its glow. Margay wasn't inside the manifestation.

Oh shit. If she wasn't here, Raz had manifested on her own. Why, for fuck's sake? Did Margay know she was here?

He lifted his cell phone and managed around a dry throat, "Siri, call Margay."

The cat half lunged at him, and Grant jumped back a pace, swinging the gun up with one hand, bracing it on his hip. The phone rang.

She picked up. "Hi, Grant." His name was a teasing purr. "In the mood for some phone sex?"

"Raz is standing three feet away from me." He managed to keep his voice calm and level. "And she's pissed."

There was an icy, electric silence. The tiger growled, low and deep, the gold of her eyes even brighter than the rest of the manifestation.

Margay spoke, her voice tight, controlled. "Grant, Raz is with me. Whoever that is, *it's not Raz.* I'm on my way."

* * *

Stark terror detonated in Margay's consciousness in concert with Raz's savage, enraged snarl. Their apartment was only three blocks away from Grant's house, but driving or running there would take minutes she didn't have.

She'd never been inside the rental -- because she'd been avoiding him like a coward -- but it was across the street from the police department. Well within the range she and Raz could project a magical manifestation. Trouble was, they couldn't manifest inside the house because they'd never *been* there. *No time to worry about that now...*

Margay and Raz reached for the hot, boiling

power of their pooled Talent and threw their melded consciousness out of her body and into the night.

They didn't even feel her human body hit the floor, out cold.

A heartbeat later, they manifested in the brick ranch's front yard and raced toward its front door. It was probably locked, but that didn't matter. They shot through the solid wood like a ghost in an old movie, solidifying the minute they were through.

The air vibrated with the deafening roar of a tiger. It didn't quite drown out Grant's furious bellow. "… going to make you into a *rug*, motherfucker!"

Margay and Raz charged through the living room and down a short hall. At the other end of it, Grant faced off with the golden blaze of the tiger, the rifle in his hands.

At the sound of Raz's roar, the other cat spun toward them.

It looked exactly like Raz.

The bastard was trying to convince Grant I tried to kill him. The thought sent fury slicing through her. Margay leaped, barreling into the tiger, who reared to meet her. They collided in an explosion of sparks and went down ripping and tearing at each other.

Pain seared her lips, her teeth, her paws as the Feral's magical field warred with her own.

But as Margay stared past the cat's translucent mask, she realized there was no human inside it.

Fuck! This is bad. Very bad.

God, the Feral was strong. She'd never seen a manifestation Raz's size glow so brightly. Could feel the cat's claws raking along her sides as she sank Raz's teeth into its throat. *Aching* to tear it apart for attacking Grant.

Unfortunately, with no physical body present,

she wouldn't be able to stop whoever sent it even if she did break the manifestation. But then, it couldn't kill her, either. And neither mani was as powerful as they'd be without a physical presence.

Then the cat's throat just vanished. Disappeared from between her teeth. Grant shouted a curse as a roar vibrated the walls. Margay whirled. The tiger had gone insubstantial and escaped to attack Grant *again*. He was scrambling to get away from it, ramming the butt of his weapon against the mani's head.

"Fucker!" she screamed, and leaped, landing on top of the manifestation just as the cat was about to go for Grant's throat. She dove for the back of its head and crunched down, raking her claws down its ribs so hard, sparks flew. Pain blazed through her senses as magic clashed with magic.

The enemy cat roared in fury and twisted...

* * *

Something slammed into Austin's face so hard, it ripped him right out of the fight. He was back in his own body, something wet rolling down his savagely aching face. His frustrated magic reverberated the air around him in a thundering roar of sheer rage.

Karl stood over him where he sat, one big fist drawn back to hit him again. "What the fuck you doing?" The big Russian demanded. "Told you not to kill cop!"

Fury and bloodlust screaming through his blood, Austin's lips peeled back from his teeth, "I don't give a fuck! Czar, *kill* the bastard!" For a moment he didn't know whether he meant the cop or the Russian. He didn't particularly care either way.

Czar lit up the house's tiny kitchen as he appeared in the blaze of a full manifestation. But instead of surrounding Austin so their joined magic could protect him, the cat stood several feet away. With a disdainful flick of his tail, the tiger turned and vanished.

I gave you an order -- go kill that fucking cop! Austin snapped at the cat. He couldn't project a manifestation that far by himself. Furious, he shut his eyes, but all he could see of the tiger was golden eyes glaring back at him through the dark. Unmoving.

Big hands clamped on his shoulders and gave him a vicious shake. "She asked you what happened, *govnosos*!"

Shit sucker? *Fuck you, asshole.* "Why the hell did you stop me?"

"Because we need cop," Anastasia snapped. "Now stand down!" Her power hit him so hard, every muscle in his body locked.

Austin roared in rage. It was all he *could* do.

This time the hand that hit his face belonged to Anastasia. The slap stung viciously. "Shut up!" she shouted. "The point of operation was not to kill cop! You were supposed to make him think you were woman's tiger! We need him to distrust her, arrest her on Bright Act! You said you could do this. *What went wrong*?"

"The pussy called her," he muttered sullenly. Anastasia's Russian accent only appeared when she was seriously pissed.

"So you fucked up, just like I said you would," Karl spat, contempt in every word.

"No, Sawyer just didn't believe Margay would send her cat to kill him. Maybe he thought she was having a nightmare or something."

"Told you this wasn't going to work," Karl said, folding his massive arms and glaring down at Austin, who still sat in the kitchen chair he'd been in when he sent his consciousness to attack Grant. "Now she knows shit-for-brains Austin is involved."

Austin wanted to manifest and rip the bastard's head off, but Czar wasn't in the mood to cooperate. "Margay doesn't know jack," he snapped. "We looked like Raz. Czar has a different stripe pattern, and he's twice the size."

"Well, she knows *some* Feral is involved. We're going back to original plan." Anastasia curled her upper lip at him.

Well, fuck. He'd argued for an hour to be allowed to attempt his idea, and the fucking cop had made him look incompetent. "I'd still kill her one on one," he said sullenly.

"Which is not the goddamn plan," Anastasia snapped. At least the American accent was back. "I may let you kill her, but not until we've caused enough chaos to distract the Americans from interfering in Ukraine."

* * *

"So there's a Feral involved in this too," Margay said grimly through Raz's manifestation. They stood in the hallway, the enemy Feral having abruptly vanished in mid-attack.

Thank God.

Grant raked a hand through his dark hair, his expression tight in the golden glow of their manifestation. "Who do you think it is?"

"No idea. That cat looked exactly like Raz, but the glow was so intense, I think it must be a male. Male tigers are twice our size, and most men are taller than I am. Their combined magic would be greater than Raz's and mine."

He frowned. "How did this guy make his manifestation look like her?"

"You can do damn near anything with a manifestation. Remember how Dad made that cat for my tenth birthday party?"

He grinned. "Some fathers do balloon animals." Hers had manifested a little margay -- the African wild cat Margay had been named for. The tiny manifestation had danced around the room collecting strokes from amazed ten-year-olds. "Darrell always did blow the curve for every other dad."

But as she watched, his smile faded, his green eyes going grim. "They tried to make me think it was you."

Knowing what she wanted -- needed -- Raz gave Margay control over their magic. The cat manifestation shrank, morphing into a copy of Margay's body rather than Raz's.

"I need to hold you," Margay said, stepping over to slide her arms around him, "and my body is on the other side of town." He stiffened in surprise at her transformation, then drew her close. Though her magical senses didn't experience the feel of him in quite the same way, she sighed at his muscular heat and solidity. *Safe. He's safe. The bastard didn't kill him.*

"This has possibilities." Grant looked down at her with a wicked grin, obviously trying to lighten the moment. "Care for a threesome?"

"What, me, you and Raz? Because I can only run one body at a time."

"Good point," he said, with an exaggerated shudder. "I'm not quite that adventurous."

"Me either." Margay combed her fingers through his hair, feeling the silky strands, seriously tempted to return to her body and drive back over to take up where they'd left off after lunch.

Except Mama would ask questions...

Margay stiffened as a horrifying realization hit. "Mama! Oh God, I left Mama alone! What if the bastard goes after her?" But if she left Grant, the bastard might try for him again. "Grant, get over to the apartment. I need everybody together before he starts trying to pick you *all* off!"

* * *

The next moment, Margay and Raz fell back into her body. She opened her eyes to see the bedroom ceiling. She shivered, feeling cold as her heart began to pound in cold panic. "Mama!"

She rolled out of bed and ran for her mother's room, throwing the door open. Her mother lay quiet and still curled up on her side. Margay rushed toward her. "Mama!" To her endless relief, Jocelyn's eyes popped open.

* * *

Blinking sleepily, her mother sat up, the blanket falling to reveal blue pajamas with a swirling snowflake pattern. "Did you have another nightmare?"

"No, this was real," Margay said grimly. "Some Feral just tried to kill Grant."

Mama's eyes rounded in horror. "*What*? What Feral? Is he all right? What happened?"

"Wait a minute, I've got to tell him you're safe." She dove for her phone and started texting. *Mom's okay. Get here as soon as you can.*

Be there in five.

"Margay," Jocelyn said through gritted teeth. "Quit torturing me and tell me what happened to Grant?"

"He called and Raz and I manifested over at his

house. There was a tiger manifestation there attacking him -- looked exactly like Raz. Same stripe pattern, same size, everything. We fought it." She frowned. "Then right in the middle of the brawl, the cat vanished. Probably decided neither one of us was going to be able to kill the other. Now Grant's on his way here to back me up -- I was afraid the creep would come after you. Mama, can he stay the night? I'm afraid the Feral's going to come back. I'll give him my bed and sleep on the couch."

"Of course." Jocelyn hesitated, eyeing her. "You know, you and Grant aren't in high school anymore. I don't expect you to pretend that you're sixteen. Just… keep it down a little." She smiled slightly. "Some things I don't need to hear."

"Oh. Uh…" Margay stared, dumbfounded.

Her mother made a little shooing gesture. "Good night, honey."

"Yeah. Yeah, good night."

"Oh, would you mind getting me a cup of that chamomile potion? I'd like to get back to sleep." Jocelyn's expression was elaborately innocent. The smile in her eyes was less so.

Margay laughed. "Sure, Mama."

* * *

The downstairs buzzer rang and she hurried down the stairs, unlocked the door and pulled it open. Grant stood on the stoop, a garment bag flung over one shoulder, and a long canvas bag in the other hand that looked as if it probably held his rifle.

"I think Mama just gave us permission to have sex," she told him.

Chapter Seven

Grant's jaw dropped as he stared at Margay in stunned surprise. "Wait, what now?"

She flashed him a cheeky grin. "I told her I'd sleep on the couch, and she told me that we weren't in high school anymore, and she saw no reason we should pretend otherwise."

He blinked as he processed that. Jocelyn was pretty religious, and he hadn't expected her to give her seal of approval to any sexual shenanigans. "Okaaaay."

"Then she told me we needed to keep it down and went back to bed."

"Yeah, that sounds like permission to me, too." Grant wasn't about to look a gift Margay in the mouth. He gave her his best wicked smile and stepped inside.

As she closed the door and locked it, Grant put the rifle case down, draped the garment bag with his clean uniforms over the banister, and reached for her as she turned to face him. Hooking one hand behind her neck beneath the soft fall of her goddess braids, he pulled her to him.

With a moan that made his hardening cock harden even more, she opened her mouth for him. He deepened the kiss, his tongue sliding along hers, stroking and tasting.

The air around them rumbled in Raz's version of a purr as Margay wrapped herself around him. Her arms encircled his neck, one long leg hooking over his hip to settle her belly against his hungry cock.

With a purring rumble of his own, he changed the angle of his mouth, deepening the kiss even more.

Margay slid her hands underneath the fabric of his sweatshirt, her blunt nails scraping over his skin.

The tickling pleasure of her touch made his heart pound and built his lust to a roar in his throbbing veins.

He'd spent so many long, lonely years thinking he'd never take her in his arms again. Feared all he'd ever have of her was a boy's memories. He'd been so damned happy when she'd come to him.

Now here she was again.

When Grant finally drew back, they were both breathing hard. "Much more of that and we'll be making love on the stairs again. Your dad almost caught us the last time."

Margay's smile drained away. "Wish he was here to do it now."

Grant winced. The death of her father -- he'd had lung cancer from his Arcane Corps service during the first Gulf war in the early 1990's -- had hit them all hard. Darrell had been a hell of a man... and more of a father to him than his own had ever been. He'd grieved for Margay's dad as he hadn't when he'd learned his sperm donor had wrapped his car around a tree. Drunk as hell. As usual. "I'm sorry. That was thoughtless."

He started to step away, but Margay grabbed his waist and held him still. "You're never thoughtless, Grant. I'm just glad you're here." Her golden eyes were wide, vulnerable. "If you hadn't called me..."

"And if you hadn't come..." Grant shook his head, remembering the cold horror when he'd tripped on the hall runner and fell on his ass. The vicious anticipation in the tiger's eyes as it gathered to spring... "You saved my life tonight. That thing would have killed me." He grimaced. "After he finished playing with me like a catnip mouse."

"I'm just glad I was in time." She studied him,

frowning. "You had a rifle, Grant. You could've used it."

"Only if I'd been willing to risk firing a high-velocity round into one of the neighbors' houses. 'Police chief accidentally kills four-year-old,' is not a headline I ever want to see."

"Good point." She managed a smile that looked a little tight. "Hate to say it, but this conversation isn't doing anything for my libido. Time to change the subject." Taking his hand in her long, warm fingers, she led him up the stairs.

As she locked the deadbolt behind them, Grant contemplated the blinking Christmas tree shedding a multicolored glow over the sectional. "Actually, the couch doesn't look that bad." His voice sounded like a purr even to himself. "And it's farther away from your mom's bedroom."

"Given that she just drank a cup of her chamomile sleeping potion, I doubt she'll come wandering out to investigate either way. She's not the one in the family who sleepwalks." Margay gave him another one of those troubled smiles, and Grant immediately resolved to drive everything but himself right out of her mind.

Catching his hand, she led him to the sectional. When she turned to him, the flashing lights of the Christmas tree painted slow, shifting patterns across her skin. He could only stare down at her, enthralled.

Something about the shape of her features reminded him of her tiger. The width of her cheekbones maybe, or the line of her nose, not to mention the Feral gold eyes that seemed to glow brighter than the Christmas tree. Her lush lips were parted, revealing white teeth. *God, she's beautiful.*

He swallowed as his gaze dropped down her

body. She wore a long white concert tee from Raven's *Feral Heart* tour, and he could see her nipples tenting the fabric. His gaze focused for a moment on the roaring tiger superimposed over the silhouette of Raven in mid-note. "Dave's head is right over your nipple. He'd love that."

"That's right, you know him." Margay flashed an evil grin. "Gonna tell him the next time you two talk?"

"Hell, no. One, he's got his own girl now. And two, I'm a selfish bastard where you're concerned." He grabbed the tee's hem and tugged it up and off. Her bare breasts bounced, sweet and tempting. Her nipples were drawn into tight little peaks, and she purred in approval as he leaned in to suck one hard tip into his mouth.

"My turn." Margay reached for the hem of his sweatshirt and dragged it upward one handed. He straightened to let her pull it off and drop it on the floor. Margay dipped her free hand to brush up his chest to seek out his own pebbled nipple. Grant inhaled sharply as she teased him.

For a moment they just stared at each other. Her skin held a lovely sheen that caught the colored light, emphasizing the ripple of feminine muscle, the curve of her waist and hips, the breasts that seemed designed to fill his hands just right. The light painted one or two scars too, and he frowned at the thought he could have lost her on one of those missions. But the Corps -- and her cat -- was just as big a part of her as his badge was of him, and he could only be grateful she'd returned to him.

His again.

Assuming she wants to be. Hope to hell she does.

When he dropped to the couch to shed his shoes and socks, Margay sat down beside him and leaned in for a gentle nibbling bite on the line of his jaw. Her long fingers danced down his bare ribs. "No tickling," he told her, trying to sound stern. Margay just grinned wickedly and dug her fingers into the spot she'd found when they were ten.

Grant growled at her, twisting around, hand lifting for a dart at his own favorite target: her taut little belly.

She fended him off with a mock pious, "Don't wake Mama."

So he grabbed her instead and dragged her close. "Wench!" He swooped in to kiss her, and she opened for him, tasting of mint toothpaste, magic and Margay.

When she eased back on the sectional, Grant braced above her, began to lick his way down the slim tendons of her throat.

With a seductive little purring croon, Margay let her head fall back, spilling braids across the seat. Her body arched against him, warm and lithe, clad only in sunflower gold panties, bare feet sliding up the legs of his jeans. His zipper dug painfully into his cock even through his boxers. *All that's got to go*, he thought, but the taste of her skin distracted him. He swirled his tongue over her banging pulse and cupped one sweet breast, strumming his thumb back and forth over its eager nipple.

"God, Grant!" Her hands tightened in his hair, pulling a little with a delightful sting.

The pressure of the zipper against his cock had grown too hard to ignore. He pulled back, laughing when she clung with that tiger strength that astonished him every time he felt it. "I need two things," he gasped. "To get you out of those panties and my balls out of these jeans before they die of strangulation."

She let him go, grinning. "Can't have that."

He stood, caught the waistband of the panties, and dragged them slowly down, watching, absorbed, as every inch of her hips and pussy were revealed. He tossed the panties aside and straightened, staring hungrily down at her. She leaned against the sectional's back, eyeing him with the same famished fascination.

Abruptly she leaned forward and freed the top snap of his jeans, then started trying to pull the zipper down. It fought her until she had to cup one hand over the bulge enough to reduce the tension. "Man, you weren't kidding." She slid onto the floor to kneel in front of him -- which didn't exactly help the problem -- as she began to peel his jeans and boxers off his hips. His erection fought her every inch of the way.

Grant balled his fists, struggling to control his libido as it bucked against his will. Until, thank God, he could step out of his jeans and kick them and his boxers aside.

Margay leaned forward, wrapping one hand around his demanding cock, and sucked its crown into her mouth. The pleasure was so incredible, he had to fight to silence a groan loud enough to overcome Jocelyn's chamomile potion.

Margay almost sabotaged the effort by sucking even more of him down, and he had to clench his teeth. She cupped his balls in gentle hands, rolling them between her fingers, her tongue dancing over exquisitely sensitive skin, each lick and slide eroding the shreds of his control.

"That's... fun," Grant panted. "But it's your turn." He bent, caught her under the arms, and swept her up onto the sectional, then scooped up her legs and hooked them over his shoulders.

"Hey! No fair!" She swatted at his shoulder in

mock offense.

"Don't care. Hi, there," Grant purred to her pouting pussy lips, spreading them with thumb and forefinger. "I missed you." And he lowered his head to take a long, juicy lick.

God, she was wet. The taste of her flooded his mouth with raw sex and magic, and he swallowed it down, his tongue dancing and skating between her swollen lips, swirling to torment her clit, then thrusting into her pussy's delicious opening.

The angle wasn't quite right, though, so he paused to scoop up one of the square black pillows and tuck it under her pretty butt. And paused, aware she was propped up on her elbows watching him.

He leaned in and flicked his tongue over the soft curls there without actually touching flesh. She rewarded him with a little hip roll. He turned his head and gave one of her thigh muscles a gentle, teasing nibble, then began nuzzling his way over to her outer lips, stopping here and there to lick, taste, bite. Not hard, just enough to make her hips roll faster.

Not yet, baby.

He reached one lip with its little crown of fluff and nestled in, taking the fine hairs between his teeth, giving them a gentle tug, then breathing into them, enjoying the rich, sensual smell.

"You…" She was panting, he realized in satisfaction. "…You've developed…"

Lick. He turned his head so he could suck the lip into his mouth. Lick…

She stopped to gasp. "…Developed a sadistic…"

Grant released the lip and took a long, long lick from perineum all the way to a quick graze of her clit.

"…Sadistic streak!" One hand clamped onto the back of his head. She didn't quite mash it against her pussy, but he could feel her considering it.

"You always did have a…" Lick. "…Hair trigger."

"I'm going to show *you* a trigger in a minute…"

"So impatient." He danced his tongue up and down for a while, circling her clit without quite touching it. Then he sealed his mouth over the nubbin's mound and suckled it hard.

She rewarded him with a squeal somewhere between orgasmic and frustrated. Raz seconded the motion with a deep rumble. "You're…playing with…fire!"

He grinned into her pussy. "I like it hot." Then he plunged his tongue into her pussy for a long, lapping stroke that made her squirm.

"Grant!" Another one of those rumbles followed, this one edging toward low roar territory.

Maybe I'd better stop fooling around… He reached up a hand for one of those soft, insanely tempting breasts and began to feast on pussy, getting his whole face in there, licking and suckling the wet, dark red flesh.

A wicked thought occurred, and he started humming, "WAP."

Her answering giggle sounded strangled. "Cardi B… would approve!" Fisting her hands in his hair again, she rolled her hips against his face, grinding shamelessly, her breath coming in short, aroused gasps.

I'm about thirty seconds from making her…

With a growl that sounded a lot more Raz than human, she jackknifed up, grabbed him beneath his arms, and lifted him right off the floor in a move that should have been impossible for anyone who weighed fifty pounds less than he did. She dropped him on his back on the cushions, rose over him on her knees, grabbed the hard length of his cock, and impaled herself in a rush.

It was Grant's turn to gasp at the sensation of slick, swollen pussy gripping his cock. It felt tight as a fist, so incredibly erotic, it was all he could do not to give a roar of his own that would wake up Jocelyn...

And every other mother in a five-mile radius.

She grinned down at him a little smugly, her gold eyes glowing, and sang a Cardi line about doing Kegels.

He stared up at her in dazed pleasure, his senses so overwhelmed that for a moment he didn't even think about anything but the way she gripped him. His brain managed a last flash of common sense, and he rasped, "Condom!"

Margay snarled like the African cat that was her namesake, her body vibrating with frustrated need. "Yeah, God knows that asshole Austin fucked around every chance he got."

Grant reached down to grope for his jeans, snagged them, and delved into a back pocket until he found the sleeve of condoms he'd added before he left home. Panting, he tore one off.

Margay grinned at them. "Confident, were you?"

"Hope springs eternal," he said, ripping the package open with his teeth.

Margay eased off him and took the condom, then began to smooth it over his cock. She took her time with it, stroking and smoothing until his control broke. It was his turn to jack upright and grab, but she dodged and crawled for the other end of the sectional.

He growled and scrambled after her, just as she draped herself over the rolled arm and looked over her shoulder at him, her gold eyes wicked and glowing with the magic of her cat. "Meow," she said, her voice so Michelle Pfeiffer throaty, he knew it was a Catwoman quote.

"Something, something, mistletoe," he managed, and was proud he had the brainpower for even that much, given her luscious, uplifted ass. Unable to resist, he bent and nuzzled in close to give her pussy another long, sensual lick. Horny as he was, she tasted delicious. He started eating her hungrily, glorying in her distilled-sex taste. Margay gasped, writhing, lushly decadent, tasting of sex and magic.

He went right on eating, determined to bring her to climax. Catching her beautiful ass cheeks in his hands, he pulled them further apart so he could get at all that slick, rosy pussy. Licking up and down, he stabbed his tongue deep, loving the way she ground against his face, straining for pleasure. The knowledge of how much he was turning her on made him even hotter.

Feeling half crazed, he went after her clit and began to suckle, sliding his middle finger up her pussy, then adding a forefinger for a grinding pump. From the corner of his eye, he saw her reach back to grab a pillow and stuff it into her mouth. "More!" Margay demanded through the muffling fabric.

Grant grinned and started in on her clit again, deep drawing sucks.

She screamed into the pillow, the muscles of her ass flexing against his hands, one foot rising to kick his shoulder as she came.

That was as much as he could take. He reared back on his knees, caught his sheathed cock, and shoved it all in right to the hilt.

"Grant!" Margay yowled into the pillow as he stroked.

He tried to go slow, he really did, but she felt so damn delicious against him, so wet and clamping, so damn perfect. He skidded right out of control and started thrusting fiercely into her.

"Yes, yes, yes!" The hot walls of her pussy tightening and releasing around him, using those impressive inner muscles to milk his shaft as he stroked in and out.

The orgasm hit him like a hot wave of dancing sparks that made him stiffen and stifle his own triumphant shout as he drowned in fire.

At last he collapsed against her sweat-slick back, bracing himself on his elbows on the arm of the sectional. He let his head fall until his cheek touched hers, her soft braids tumbling over his shoulder as he wrapped his arms around her. Losing himself in the sweet peace of the moment, he listened to her breathe.

* * *

It took a while for them to collect the ambition to rearrange themselves, Grant reclining into the sectional, Margay curling into his arms. He lay floating, higher than any addict, watching the way the Christmas tree lights gleamed on the light sweat glazing her lush body. Sleepily, he traced swirling patterns on her skin, his mind for once blank.

But just as he started drifting off to sleep, she stirred to slide him a lazy smile. "We'd better get dressed and go to my room. I don't think we want to scandalize Mama with the sight of a naked white boy when she comes out to cook breakfast in the morning."

Grant laughed softly. "Good point."

They dressed a lot more slowly than they'd undressed, then headed for her room.

* * *

Jimmy Miller swaggered into Six Shooters on his meal break, planning to grab a burger and fries.

It was going to be another excruciatingly boring shift, driving around looking for trouble. Probably wouldn't find a goddamn thing.

Maybe that Feral bitch would go running again tonight. He loved driving behind her with his headlights lighting up her long legs and tight, sexy little ass. She'd get all tense, obviously worrying what he might do. He loved the fuck out of that.

Maybe he'd get out and harass her, try to start something. See if he could set her off.

Buuuut… maybe that's not a good idea. He'd seen that video on the news. The glowing tiger crouched and snarling, ears laid back, sparks and magical smoke boiling off it like she was a fucking Marvel character come to life.

He'd watched helmet cam video on YouTube once -- two manifestations fighting during the war -- but he'd always figured it was a government fake, nothing but special effects.

But WSAG didn't have the budget for that kind of shit. Plus, everybody in town was talking about it. Aunt Carol had been at the Spoon and seen the tiger, huge and throwing off more sparks than those firecrackers. "I thought I was cat kibble for sure," she'd told his mom, who'd told him. "But Jocelyn and the chief talked Margay down. We'd have all been dead otherwise."

The Feral bitch had been home for months without anybody seeing her tiger. He'd figured Old Lady Whitfield was lying -- that she didn't even *have* a tiger. Maybe a dog or something. Maybe a poodle, one of those little yappy ones. Why would they give a tiger to a *woman*?

But *that* thing…

He'd gotten out of the car with her just last week -- not to hurt her, just to fuck with her a little. He'd have kept his ass in the car if he'd had any idea. Christ, that monster could have ripped him apart!

No, better not mess with her tonight even if she did show up. Never mind that the chief had a thing for her, and Jimmy loved nothing more than to get one up on that bastard.

I should've been chief. Been policing in this one-stoplight town for two years now. I deserve a promotion, damn it. A raise. He could've done the job.

His uncle had turned him down flat. "*You ain't exactly a rocket surgeon, boy,*" Uncle Sean had told him. "*Especially not next to Grant Sawyer. Hell, he helped save the* president. *This town is lucky to get him, especially with him being a national hero.*"

Talk about your bullshit. Sawyer only cracked that case because of his furry buddies Kurt and Jake and their witch whore. Jimmy could have done as well with a pair of Ferals watching *his* back. But nobody in the family gave him credit for shit.

Especially not his dad. "*You're a fuckup, Jimmy!*" All the time he was growing up, that's all he ever heard from dear old Dad. Didn't make the football team. "*You're a fuckup, Jimmy!*" Had to repeat twelfth grade and didn't get to graduate with his class. "*You're a fuckup, Jimmy!*"

He ignored the inner voice that always asked, *What if Dad's right?*

He goddamn was *not* right.

One day Jimmy would show them. He'd show every last one of them what he could do. Starting with that Affirmative Action Queen, Margay, *and* her pet pussycat.

God, he wanted a beer. But the chief had said if he ever heard of Jimmy being drunk on the job, he was gone. And he wasn't sure Uncle Sean would lift a finger to save him.

The creak of the bar door opening distracted Jimmy from his brooding with a blast of icy air. He looked around in annoyance...

Just as the woman walked in.

Jimmy felt his jaw drop. *Christ, she's gorgeous.* Must be passing through because he'd never seen her before. *But hot fuck, I wish I had...*

The woman's gaze swept over the restaurant, and their stares collided. Jimmy could feel himself getting hard. He couldn't help it. She just had that *look* -- the kind that made you think about pretty red mouths wrapped around your cock.

Except then her gaze flicked away, and she sauntered past, her lush ass rolling.

Jimmy stared after her, entranced. He'd buy her a drink, see if he could get lucky. Maybe he could even get a quickie before she left to go back to wherever she came from.

After all, women loved cops.

* * *

As Margay and Grant cuddled in her bed, a series of uncomfortable thoughts began to float up from her subconscious.

Suddenly she didn't feel sleepy in the least. "You know, this isn't just some Arcanist pulling the shit," Margay told him. "This is a Feral. And he's got power. His manifestation was blazing like a spotlight."

Grant nodded grimly. "And what if the bastard goes after your mom next?"

"Yeah." *Mama wouldn't have had a prayer.*

At least Grant had been able to hold the prick off long enough for Margay to get to him.

Yet he'd thanked her for saving his life without even a trace of offended ego.

A memory flashed through her mind -- Austin, stunned when artillery had exploded too close to their position. Margay had been fully manifested, but he hadn't been -- playing fearless again, something he'd done entirely too often. She and Raz had swept him up in her manifestation and carried him to safety, bounding into a nearby trench.

When Austin recovered his senses, not only had he *not* thanked her, he'd been an absolute shit about the entire thing. During the resulting row, he'd snarled, "I guess you think you're some kind of hot shit hero, but I've got news for you. Without that cat, you're nothing."

That had been the moment when he'd started to pull away. By the time they were training that last batch of recruits, it was obvious he was cheating on her.

As if to make sure she knew it, Austin had made a point of getting close to her whenever he came back from his excursions off the base. He'd known Raz's sensitive nose would pick up the scent of another woman.

And what had triggered it all was that rescue.

Just proves he's completely different from Grant. Grant thanked me.

But that set the wheels in motion, a paranoid little voice whispered in the depths of her mind. *What if Grant starts resenting me too?*

RRRmmmmmph, Raz rumbled, sounding disgusted. And not at Grant.

In the next heartbeat, the cat appeared fully

manifested, so close her whiskers brushed Grant's face. He jerked and almost bolted away. Margay tightened her grip on the arms he'd wrapped around her waist, holding him still. "It's just Raz showing she loves you."

"By giving me a heart attack?" He sank down behind her again, eyeing the cat. Raz extended her head again, sniffing.

"Go ahead and pet her," Margay told him. "She loves you." *Because I do*, she thought, but didn't say out loud.

She frowned, realizing Raz's trick just now was exactly the kind of bullshit that would have sent Austin into a cursing, embarrassed fury.

Which was probably exactly the point the tiger had been trying to make. Raz might not have the ability to speak in words, but she had better instincts when it came to people than Margay did.

Raz would never have gotten involved with Austin Fucking Reynolds to begin with.

Mrrrophph, the tiger agreed, a little smugly.

Then, of course, her inner neurotic had to chime in. Because of course it did. *No matter how much Grant loves you, he's still a guy. Guys don't like women who can outmuscle them -- the way you did when you forgot yourself.*

Shut. Up.

Grant and Raz were still staring at one another. Hesitantly, he reached out a hand and stroked his fingers through her fur.

"She loves scratches behind the ears," Margay told him. "Just like any house cat." *See? We're not that scary.*

"She feels real," he said, his tone wondering. "How the hell does that work? She's actually *made out of magic*. I tried to watch this YouTube thing about manifestations, but these physicists were talking about quantum fields and magical quarks and all kinds of crap which made no goddamn sense whatsoever."

"Yeah, I think I know the video you mean, and I didn't understand it either," Margay told him. "Look, the truth is, she feels real because she *is* real. Because I remember what her fur felt like, just like she remembers how it feels to be petted. We draw on those memories when we create the manifestation."

He dug his fingers into her thick fur, scratching harder, and Raz rumbled, angling her head so he could hit exactly the right spot. "You're amazing," he told the cat. "And so goddamn gorgeous."

Margay smiled, relaxing again at the wonder in his voice. The fear was gone from his scent now, leaving behind only the clean scent of wonder. There was no trace of resentment or anger at all.

Grant really was as far from Austin as it was possible to get. As far from the norm men she'd encountered in the military who'd viewed her with resentment because of her greater-than-human strength.

Even norm officers had treated her with wariness, as if she were a hand grenade that might go off at any moment.

Grant did not treat her that way, even though she almost had gone off on him.

As if sensing her mood, he dipped his head to better see her face, frowning. "What's wrong?"

"Nothing."

He studied her with those acute green eyes. "Yeah, calling bullshit on that. When a woman says 'nothing' in that tone, it's always something." He grimaced, and she scented pain.

"Speaking from personal experience?"

"Yeah, it starts with 'I'm fine,' and ends with

divorce papers." Then he shook off the mood and changed the subject. "So I got some interesting witness statements today about that damn box."

Margay pulled out of his grip so she could look at him. "Did someone see the asshole plant the MEED?"

"Unfortunately, no. But they did see something even better. Remember our fourth-grade teacher, Mrs. Jones?"

"Oh, yeah. I love her. She's a regular at the Spoon. In fact, I saw her today when I was bussing tables. She stopped me to ask how I was doing."

"Any idea what time she arrived?"

Margay frowned. "I wasn't in the dining room when she came in, but I did speak to her about… I don't know, twenty minutes before the bomb went off. Something like that, anyway."

"She said she could see behind the counter before the fireworks went off and there was no sign of anything there. When my mother called yours to the phone, Mrs. Jones was looking right at the box. First, there was nothing there, but she saw it appear for a second or two before the fireworks blew it apart. Which suggests you're right and it was invisible. Think she really had a view of it? Sometimes witnesses exaggerate."

"She wasn't exaggerating. She was in the booth right across from the Square station on the counter. She'd have had a good view, assuming Mama and Nancy weren't in the way. There's not much room back there."

"Apparently when they tripped, she saw the box." He stroked one hand up and down Margay's upper arm, the gesture pensive. "So we've got a suspect who's a Feral, who's working with both an

Arcanist and an Alchemist."

"Maybe," Margay said. "Or maybe he hired somebody to create the MEED *and* the potion."

"Either way he's definitely targeting you. Any idea who this guy is? Assuming it's a guy. You did say women with tiger Familiars aren't that common."

"I'm pretty sure it's a guy, probably with a male tiger, just in terms of the sheer power that manifestation had. A female team wouldn't have been able to generate that much juice because their combined weight isn't that great. And it's weight that counts when it comes to a meld's magic."

"But why did he make his cat look like Raz? And how did he know what she looks like?"

"Yeah, he even got the stripes right. What I don't understand is why he kept up the masquerade after I attacked him. A male tiger would've had the advantage against Raz."

"Not if he thought you'd recognize his cat," Grant pointed out. "Which implies you know this asshole."

Margay considered the idea and shook her head. "But I can't think who'd want me dead, except a few Caliphate sorcerers and the Russians." She winced a little. "I did *not* say that. And don't ask."

Grant frowned at her. "Do you seriously think that I'm going to run to the media and tattle?"

"Some shit is top-secret for a reason."

"And sometimes the reason is it would embarrass the government."

Margay set her jaw. "This is not one of those times. I don't want to hand the Humanist Party a brick to beat the Constitutionalists with."

He eyed her. "Okay, have it your way. Who knows you well enough to duplicate Razia's stripe pattern?"

"Plenty of people in the Corps."

"How about that guy you were dating? Mom said there was somebody -- Austin something."

"Austin Reynolds, and yeah, he'd be able to do it. God knows he is an asshole, but being an asshole doesn't mean you'd do something like this."

"When I was with the Laurelton Sheriff's Office, I investigated plenty of assholes who tried to kill women they were involved with. And a lot of them succeeded. There's one in Ashburg now I'm keeping a damn close eye on."

"Point," Margay admitted, absently stroking his biceps much the way he'd petted Raz. "But someone who does that kind of shit is obsessed with the woman. Either he's married to her, or they're living together, or he thinks she belongs to him for some reason. Austin and I never had that kind of relationship. We were at best fuck buddies."

She felt the muscles in his arm tighten, then slowly relax as if he were fighting a wave of jealousy. To her disgust, that thought gave her a pleasant little thrill. She ignored it. "And it was Austin who broke it off. Anyway, when it comes to the stripe pattern, the Corps keeps records of that kind of thing. A tiger's stripes are just like a fingerprint, so it's a way to ID the animal. They do the same thing with lions' manes and biometrics on bear Familiars. If somebody hacked into those files, they could duplicate the stripe pattern even if they'd never seen Raz."

"Could it be the same person who did that MEED bombing in…" His mouth twisted. "…Wherever it is you're not allowed to talk about."

"Yeah," she said slowly. "But again, why?"

"The Russians don't like you very much?"

Oh, hell, that horse is not only out of the barn, he's running in the Kentucky Derby. There's no real point in pretending otherwise.

But still.

Grant eyed her, then continued, "I think we need to look at this Austin asshole. Where is he?"

Margay shrugged. "I have no idea. Probably in the States somewhere. He's in the same boat I'm in. His cat died too, so he's probably in therapy. Once he can prove to the Corps that he and Czar are stable, he can go back on active duty. And I'm inclined to think he will. I've always had the impression he took a good chunk of his identity from being in the Corps."

Grant studied her. "Are you going to go back on active duty?"

"No. I'm done with that. Getting shot at isn't as much fun as *Call Of Duty* makes it look. And getting blown up isn't a party, either." She grimaced. "Especially when you're doing it for people who actively hate you."

"The Ukrainians hated you?"

"No, but the Humanists sure as fuck do. And every time they get a government majority, they become an existential threat to me, my mom and anybody else with a lick of Talent." *Besides,* she thought, *you're here. And now you and I have a chance.*

Which reminded her of something that had been niggling in her subconscious for months. "One thing I don't get, Grant. You were involved in cases that got national attention. Given your resume, you could have done better than chief of a seven-man department that's chronically shorthanded. You could be making six figures somewhere a lot bigger than Ashburg. Why here?"

He looked at her. "You really have to ask?"

Margay felt her jaw drop. "But I was still in the Corps when you took this job."

"And you came home every leave." Grant reached out and took her hand. "I hoped I'd have an opportunity to mend the fences I broke by marrying Brandy. And when your mom told my mom you were fighting with Austin, it dawned on me you'd had ten years of running around with other Ferals, but you hadn't settled down with any of them." He looked down at her hands, toying with her fingers, stroking his thumb over her blunt, unpolished nails. "But when you came back, you wouldn't even speak to me. And I was worried about you. I've known people with PTSD. After the Faraday Square massacre, we had a guy who committed suicide. Another guy, Sergeant Johnson, he was so fucked up about it, he got involved with Virginia Laurel and her terrorist plot. He's doing time now."

"Grant, I'm not going to start committing crimes," she told him, turning her hand to clasp his. "And I'm not going to commit suicide either."

He looked up at her. "That's not what I was implying. I just meant… The truth is, the massacre fucked me up too. I still have nightmares about that day. Watching that polar bear kill that cop…" He tightened his grip on her hand and sighed. "And then there was that goddamn riot. There are nights the two of them alternate. I wake up with one, have to drug myself back to sleep with a sleeping pill, then promptly have the other one."

"Yeah, sometimes I do the same thing." She reached up and threaded her fingers through his hair. "Sounds like I'm not the only one who needs therapy."

"Yeah, probably. But nobody wants to give a gun to a cop who's seeing a therapist."

He turned fully to her, his green gaze level and rock steady. "I love you, Margay. I've loved you since I was fifteen, and that never changed. Not even after a decade apart. It's not *going* to change. If you don't want to be with me, that's your choice. But you're always going to be half my heart."

Her eyes were stinging now, and she felt a tear break loose and roll down her face. "Oh God, I love you, too." She cupped his cheek in her hand. "But sometimes it takes more than love to make it."

Chapter Eight

That night, Jimmy drove around his patrol zone, his hands tight on the unit's wheel, angry excitement sizzling through him with every beat of his heart.

He stopped at a stop sign, pulled out his phone and searched his contacts for the next guy on his list.

"Hey, Clay," he said.

His friend answered in a sleep-drugged whine. "Jimmy, for fuck's sake, I have to go to work in the morning!"

"This is more important."

"Yeah, well, unlike you, I have a wife and kid."

"And if you don't want them to be tiger chow, maybe you'd better goddamn pay attention."

"The fuck are you talking about?"

"Did you see the video? That bitch almost ate everybody in the restaurant! She's dangerous! We've got to do something about her before it's too late."

"Jesus, Jimmy, you always said she didn't even have a tiger. Said it was probably one of those toy poodles…"

"Well, she's got a tiger. I don't know who she blew to get it, but she's got a tiger. And we need to do something about her. Her, and that mother of hers. One of these days that bitch Jocelyn is going to poison everybody in town." He snorted. "The Arcane Corps? Ha! Should call it the Satan Corps. That's how they get those cats to begin with. Probably sacrifice babies or something."

"Jimmy, you are *so* full of shit." He hung up.

Jimmy shrugged and sent Clay's contact to his new friend. She'd make the guy see reason. She'd get everybody just where they needed to be.

She was real good at that.

* * *

Anastasia walked into the Morning Scramble at five a.m. The Scramble was the kind of greasy spoon that mainly catered to truckers, and the waitstaff looked a little confused at the number of people packing it at this hour.

Anastasia could be very persuasive when she wanted to be.

This would be just the first little meeting she'd hold today. By the time she got done talking, the owner would lose that confused and wary look. He'd be all in.

Anastasia stood up from the tables Jimmy's friends had pushed together. As the crowd watched her with skeptical eyes, she drew in a breath.

And began to sing, "God Bless America."

That was a nice touch if she did say so herself. By the time the last piercing note had faded, she owned everyone in the restaurant.

* * *

It was nine o'clock in the morning when it started. Margay, Nancy, and the rest of the Spoon crew were busy cleaning up the mess from the day before, Grant having released the scene back to them.

They'd cleared all the tables and gone to work cleaning the prep areas. Now, while the crew swept, mopped, and hauled off trash, Margay got everything ready for the Hobart dishwasher.

In the distance, she heard a shout, followed by the rumble of loud, angry voices.

What the hell is that? Calling on Razia's keen hearing, she concentrated.

From the sound of it, a bunch of people were

congregating outside the restaurant. And they weren't happy about something. "Hey, Mama," she called to Jocelyn, who was cleaning a nearby prep station, "I think we've got a problem. Sounds like a crowd's gathering outside."

Margay dried her hands and headed into the dining room, her mother at her heels, trailed by Nancy, Brenda and the Alchemists, Shanna Prince and Joe Jeffries.

Sure enough, a crowd had assembled on the sidewalk outside the plate-glass windows. Many carried poster board signs duct-taped to sticks. Black magic marker spelled out, "Satanists are not welcome here!" and "No witches in Ashburg!"

One muscular, angry young man held a sign that said, "Thou shalt not suffer a witch to live!"

"Oh, hell," Shanna moaned, eyes widening. She was a short, tattooed thirty-year-old who was almost as good with herbal magic as Jocelyn. "They're quoting Exodus. That's never good."

"Time to nip that in the bud." Margay headed for the front door, Raz's growl rumbling in the air around her, savage with threat.

"Margay, don't!" Her mother latched onto her forearm. Margay pulled free, but Jocelyn grabbed her again as Nancy caught the other shoulder.

"No!" Mama snapped. "If you go out there, you'll have to manifest to get rid of them and that's just going to pour gasoline all over this."

"Yeah," Nancy added. "And you don't want to violate the Bright Act, because Grant would have to bust you."

Margay stopped, staring from one woman to the other as the full implications hit her. "This is because of me. This is because I lost it yesterday."

"Call Grant," Mama urged. "Have *him* get these people out of here. I doubt they've got a permit, not that the mayor would give them one for a Main Street business that's been the town's only tourist attraction for years."

"God bless *Magical Kitchens*," Margay muttered, and pulled her cell out of her apron pocket. "Siri, call Grant."

He picked up on the first ring. "Hey, Margay," he said, his voice low and intimate.

Too bad she had to ruin the mood. "Grant, we've got a problem." Glancing out the window, she realized many of the people out there were regulars. Her stomach sank even deeper. *What the fuck have I done?* "There's a mob of protestors outside the Spoon. They've got signs and they're chanting. And one of the signs mentions Exodus 22:18." Every Talent knew that chapter and verse.

Grant swore. "That goddamn video on the morning news." They'd watched it this morning before he went to work.

"And that's not even mentioning the reposts on YouTube and Facebook. Plus sheer first-hand experience on the part of everyone who was there," she agreed. "I recognize a bunch of them from yesterday." Her eyes began to sting. "Jesus, Grant, what the hell did I do?"

His voice sharpened. "You didn't do anything. You didn't hurt anybody. Let's keep it that way. Stay inside and I'll take care of it."

He hung up, and Margay returned to staring out the window at the shouting, angry faces of the crowd. None of them looked like they were willing to listen to reason.

"Oh, man," Nancy moaned. "This isn't good. Not

at all."

"Yeah, we're screwed," Joe Jeffries said glumly. The grizzled old Alc had worked for the Spoon since Margay's grandmother hired him.

The crowd began to chant, "Thou Shalt Not Suffer a Witch…"

* * *

As much as Grant wanted to charge in and kick ass, he couldn't Lone Ranger a riot. Especially not if the protest was legal. So he called the mayor's office, which was located in the same slate gray converted high school as the Ashburg PD.

The town clerk confirmed that nobody had issued a permit to picket the Spoon.

Well, it was something, anyway. Grant strode from the building and headed for his unit, only to stop in mid-step, frowning.

Even from three blocks away, he could hear the rumble of angry voices.

"Shit." He fobbed the Interceptor open and slid in, hitting his lights and sirens before pulling out. As he roared for the Spoon, he radioed dispatch and told them to call in the off-duty officers for backup. He needed them, since Roger was halfway to Columbia by now, transporting the MEED evidence to the state Arcane lab.

But Christ, he hoped not. This was Ashburg. Grant had grown up with these people, and he couldn't believe they'd go after cops. It's not like they were Human Heritage, for God's sake…

Or at least, he hoped not, because it might take time for the off-duty cops to arrive. *Assuming they even show up at all. Jimmy, you sheep-fucking asshole, I'm going to fire you if you don't.*

When he hit the intersection two blocks later, there was indeed a crowd jostling sullenly in front of the Spoon. And every damned one of them looked incredibly pissed-off.

Looks like more than fifty people. This could be bad. If backup doesn't show, I'm fucked.

He parked his SUV blocking the intersection, blue lights flashing. Which was when he spotted the news van sitting by the curb. A reporter and his cameraman were interviewing protesters.

Oh, great, just what we need, Grant thought, grabbing the bullhorn he'd brought and sliding out of the SUV. He stalked toward the protestors.

Usually with groups like this, they formed a ring and marched in a circle yelling their grievances. This bunch was clustered right at the Spoon's plate-glass window, screaming at the staff inside.

"Witch! Poisoner!"

"Satanist!"

Grant raised the bullhorn and triggered it. "Ashburg Police! This is an illegal protest. You don't have a permit. If you want to march, disperse and get one."

Nobody even turned around, too busy yelling at Margay and her mother through the glass. Grant raised the volume on the bullhorn and triggered it again. "I want to see your permit right now!" Sounding electronic and menacing, his amplified voice rang out over the shouts. "Otherwise, this is an illegal demonstration. If you don't disperse, *somebody's going to jail!*"

Now members of the crowd turned. For a moment he thought they were all strangers until he realized their faces were twisted with such hate and blind fury, he hadn't even recognized them.

This reminded him way too much of the Laurel Park riot three years before. Human Heritage loons under the influence of bespelled vodka had attacked Laurel County Sheriff's deputies and South Carolina Highway Patrol troopers, along with cops from surrounding jurisdictions.

He'd been one of those cops.

At one point, Grant had honestly believed he wasn't going to survive the riot. Four Human Heritage thugs had jumped him and beaten him badly. He'd fought back with everything he had, making ruthless use of his asp baton and pepper spray. His gun had stayed in its holster. He'd known if he opened fire, they'd tear him apart.

Then somebody sucker punched him, and he'd gone down. They'd been kicking him when Jake, fully manifested, leaped into the scrum and scattered them like a cat among pigeons.

As it was, Grant had gone to the ER with a concussion and broken ribs. He'd been lucky -- a cop and two protesters had been killed outright. There'd been a thousand injuries, some critical.

Now that memory made his heartbeat spike and his peripheral vision narrow. The rioters' shouts took on a metallic quality. Distant sirens approached, and the sound sent a burst of relief through him. He just had to stall until help arrived. "Do not test me," he snarled through the bullhorn. "If you do not disperse, you're all going to need lawyers -- and *you'll be cooling your heels in the county jail*!"

"Why are you sticking up for the witches?" a woman screeched. "Traitor!"

"I said disperse!" he thundered through the bullhorn.

"Why haven't you arrested that Feral creature for

violating the Bright Act?" Belatedly, Grant recognized the speaker as his mother's pastor. He stared, incredulous. The man had never been anti-Talent before. And he'd called Margay a creature?

"I don't care if you did date Margay in high school," an old woman with blue hair shouted. "That bitch is demon-possessed! She needs to be locked up before she kills somebody!"

Jesus, it's Mrs. Jones, Grant realized. *What set her off? She was on Margay's side yesterday.* "Disp…"

"They're playing you! There was no bomber!" Mrs. Jones screamed, shoving through the crowd to lurch toward him. Bizarrely, his old teacher wore red slacks and a Christmas sweater with Rudolf on it. The reindeer's LED nose blinked red, a cheerful note at complete odds with her crazed blue gaze. "I saw Margay Whitfield plant that box of firecrackers myself!"

Grant stared at her, so surprised he forgot trying to reason with a rioter is a waste of time. "Yesterday you said you didn't even *see* the box until it blew up."

"Liar! I said no such thing!" Mrs. Jones lunged at him, frail hands curled into claws.

Grant sidestepped and caught her shoulders before she could fall on her face. "Mrs. Jones, you're going to get hurt."

"Traitor!" The crowd lurched toward him, fists drawn back, faces contorted. None of them looked anything like the friends and neighbors he'd known for years.

Something raked hard across his jaw. "Animal fucker!" the old woman screeched, and went for his eyes with her nails.

"What's wrong with you?" he demanded, fending off her hands. *This has* got *to be a spell. Who the hell cast it? How do I break it? There isn't an Arcanist for miles -- except for the asshole who cast this.*

A patrol unit roared around the corner and screeched to a stop. Corporal Tom Keller of Charlie shift jumped out with a huge canister of CAP-STUN pepper spray. "Have you people lost your damn minds? Back off, this is an illegal protest!"

A dozen people charged him as the rest of the mob headed for Grant. Keller hosed them down with the canister, sending them stumbling back, blinded.

Grant swung Mrs. Jones out of the way, gave her a little push, and spun to block a punch from his mom's preacher. A vicious kick landed on the back of his calf, but he ignored it. *Must've come from Mrs. Jones.*

A fist rammed into the side of his head so hard he staggered. He grabbed the pepper spray off his belt and fired it right in the face of his attacker -- a middle-aged man he didn't recognize. The man recoiled, bellowing.

A tiger roared!

Another echoed it somewhere to the right, followed immediately by a third roaring from around the corner. A fourth joined in, the cats' voices merging into a chorus of terrifying sonic blasts that seemed to come from all around them. Sounded like an entire pack of tigers were closing in. *What the hell?*

For a moment, the whole crowd froze, then whirled and scattered, their screams almost drowned out by the deafening roars.

A woman and two men ran right into Grant, the impact driving him into Mrs. Jones. He felt her start to fall and grabbed her. Off-balance, he went down with her, instinctively shielding the old woman's head with his forearms as his elbows slammed painfully to the pavement. Feet hit his back, and he braced himself, trying not to let his weight crush her. She clung to him, screeching in terror.

Finally, the screams faded, and Grant pushed off his former teacher. Even the tigers shut up. "Are you okay?"

Mrs. Jones gave him a dazed blink, obviously not tracking. "What?"

Grant glanced toward the Spoon to see Margay hurrying toward him. "Hey, are you okay?" she gasped.

"Just some bruises." His eyes widened as the light dawned. "I gather you're responsible for the enraged tiger sound effects?" He'd seen Dave do the same kind of magical ventriloquist act.

She grinned. "Didn't want to get busted on the Bright Act."

He grimaced. "Thank you for making sure I don't have to arrest you." Sighing, he reached for his radio handset to call for an ambulance.

Corporal Keller walked up. Keller was pushing forty, a lean, silver-haired man, who, with Roger, was one of Grant's go-to guys in the department. "What the hell was that about?"

"Somebody using their powers for evil," Margay told him. "I could literally see the magic hanging in the air around those people."

* * *

Margay bent, intending to help Grant assist lift Mrs. Jones to her feet, but the old woman cowered away from her in terror. "Don't eat me!"

She froze, staring and appalled. "I would never hurt you, Mrs. Jones. I didn't hurt anyone yesterday either, despite the MEED…"

"I saw you plant that box! How could you do

something like that?"

"What? I didn't…"

Grant held up a hand, and Margay fell silent. "Mrs. Jones, that's not what you told me yesterday. You said the box was invisible. It only appeared when the fireworks went off."

"I did not! Why are you lying?"

Grant pulled his cell phone from its clip and did some swiping. A moment later Mrs. Jones's voice emerged from his phone. "I was sitting in the booth across from checkout, and I had a good view behind that counter. When Nancy called Jocelyn to the phone, I glanced over. There was nothing there. When the first pop went off, it looked like the light from the fireworks just appeared in midair. Jocelyn and Nancy leaped away -- I think Jocelyn got burned -- and they both tripped and went down. I jumped up and saw a box just… appear out of nowhere. A minute later, the explosions blew it apart. The pieces flew everywhere."

The old woman stared at the phone in surprise and fear. "That's… that's not me!"

"It *is* you, Mrs. Jones," Grant told her gently. "This is the recording I made when I spoke to you in the beauty shop yesterday."

"I wasn't at the beauty shop!"

"Mrs. Jones, your hair's blue," his mother put in, walking up to join them. "It was silver when I saw you at lunch yesterday."

"It is *not*!"

Gently, Nancy caught a lock of the old woman's hair and pulled it out so she could see it. "See? Blue."

Mrs. Jones stared at it, her mouth working in confusion. "Oh. I did see that this morning and I… I forgot." Her face crumpled in fear and bewilderment. "Am I getting Alzheimer's?"

"No," Margay said firmly. "You're sharp as a tack. You're also under a spell. Did you talk to any strangers?"

"No." She bit her lip. "At least, I don't think so."

"Chief Sawyer?"

Margay looked up just as Darius Palmer with WSAG shoved a mic in Grant's face. "Are you going to arrest Margay Whitfield for manifesting?"

"I didn't manifest," Margay interrupted, thoroughly sick of the reporter's crap. "All I did was roar."

Palmer curled a handsome lip in a sneer. "A human throat did not make those sounds."

Margay looked at him and crossed her arms. A chorus of roars so loud Grant felt them in his sternum erupted in the air. Mrs. Jones gave a little scream and cowered into Nancy's arms. Both Palmer and his cameraman jumped.

"You know better than that," Margay told the reporter when the echo faded. "How do you think Dave Frost does a standup act in the body of a tiger?"

"But..."

She refused to let him finish. "*I did not manifest. I* just used magic to make the air vibrate, which is not illegal. Just like everybody else, I have freedom of speech. Mine is just louder."

Palmer glowered at her, then turned to his videographer. "Did you get a video of her manifesting?"

The woman shook her head. "She didn't manifest. She just stuck her head outside the restaurant door, and it sounded like every tiger on the planet lost its damn mind. Didn't even open her mouth. No glowing Tiger, no nothing."

The reporter visibly ground his teeth as he glared

daggers at Margay before turning to Grant again. "So you think these people are under a spell?"

"Yeah, because I know them. They're not the type to form a mob and run amok. I went to school with half of them, and I trick-or-treated at the other half's homes when I was a kid."

"They've never acted like this before," Margay agreed.

"Don't you think it could have something to do with the fact that you manifested and scared everyone?" Palmer demanded. "When you terrorize people, they get angry."

"The word 'terrorize' implies I did it on purpose," Margay said. "I'm a combat veteran, and someone went to a lot of trouble to give me a flashback to an explosion that killed my tiger. I controlled my Familiar, but I did roar at people and frighten them yesterday. I genuinely regret that. But I didn't do it intentionally."

"My daughter fought for this country, and she almost died doing it." Jocelyn hurried up, carrying the shadow box that usually hung in Margay's room. "Look here." She shoved the box at the videographer. "That's a Silver Star," she said, pointing at one of the medals. "That's the Arcane Corps' Bronze Lion, that's a Pentagram for Gallantry. And that one is the Purple Heart." She turned a ferocious glare on Palmer. "My daughter doesn't deserve to get treated by like garbage by opportunistic politicians -- or reporters."

Grant must have decided that was his cue to end the conversation. "No further comment," he said firmly, and started herding the women back to the restaurant.

* * *

While Grant sent Tom Keller home -- he'd been off duty -- and canceled the call for additional backup, the women helped Mrs. Jones into a booth to wait for the ambulance. The old woman huddled there, looking pale and frightened.

"Would you like some tea?" Jocelyn asked. "And we've got cookies. I think you could probably stand to get your blood sugar up a little bit. That's quite a bump on your head." She stretched out a hand, but Mrs. Jones shied back, her eyes widening. Jocelyn arrested the gesture and said, "I can make you a nice cup of chamomile."

Blue eyes flickered nervously. "No, thank you."

Jocelyn drew back and asked quietly, "Louise, do you honestly believe I'd put a spell on you, much less poison you? You taught my daughter. You've been my customer for years. Have I ever done anything to make you think I misuse my magic?"

"No, but…" Mrs. Jones knotted her thin hands together. "Maybe I just didn't notice."

Jocelyn started to turn away, only to pause and square her shoulders. Without turning, she asked, "Would you drink a glass of tap water? You look dehydrated, and your color isn't good."

"I'll get it," Nancy said. "Everybody knows I don't have magic. I'll pour it out of the tap." She looked at the rest of the crew. "Anybody want anything? Coffee?"

"God, yes." Grant sat down across from the old woman. "Who told you that Jocelyn poisons people?"

Mrs. Jones looked down at her hands. The line of her shoulders was tight. "I think maybe I'd better go home."

"I'm not going to let anyone hurt you, ma'am," Grant told her. "I think I demonstrated that today."

She looked up at him and blinked, her confused gaze seeming to sharpen. "You shielded me. Those people ran over the top of you -- right across your back, but you protected me. Covered my head with your arms when we fell."

"Yes, I did."

"If they'd stepped on *me* like that, they might've broken bones. I have osteoporosis." Mrs. Jones sagged, shaking her head. "Why am I even here? Why did I come to this... this protest or whatever it was? That was stupid. None of us should have been here -- somebody could have been badly hurt. She's a *tiger*."

"Do you mind if I record this?" Grant asked, pulling out his cell phone.

She hesitated, eyeing him. "Are you going to arrest me?"

"No. None of this is your fault."

"I guess it's all right, then."

"Can you tell me what you did today?"

"Well, I came to join the protest."

"How did you find out there was going to be a protest?"

"I got a call."

"Do you know who called you?"

Mrs. Jones frowned. "I don't... I didn't recognize the voice."

"Could you describe the caller?"

"It was a woman, I think. She said it was time to take the town back from the witches and the Satanists. Otherwise, people are going to start dying. Margay was going to..." She looked up at Margay, who stood looking out the window at Main Street.

"Margay was going to do what?" Grant asked, keeping his tone calm, gentle. "What did she say Margay was going to do?"

Mrs. Jones frowned deeply. "She was going to eat people."

Despite the sting of temper, he asked, "Has she ever eaten anyone before?"

"No." Louise Jones's seamed face pulled into a frown. "Why would I think she was going to eat someone? Margay's always been a good girl. She gave me the most delicious orange pound cake for Christmas the year I taught y'all. That cake was so good, I wanted to give her an A." She smiled a little. "Fortunately, she deserved one."

Louise fell silent, frowning in concentration, then shook her bright blue head. "None of this makes sense. Why would I come to a protest when she said there was going to be violence? I'm not like that." She lifted a hand and probed the bruise on her forehead. Winced. "I'll be lucky if I don't have a concussion. I could've died. If you hadn't caught me the way you did, they'd have trampled me." The old woman bit her lower lip. "But I saw Margay put that box on the floor behind the counter."

"Did you say anything about it to her?"

"No. Seems like I would've, doesn't it?" She touched the bump on her head again. "Would you play that recording again?"

He found the recording, then thumbed play. Louise's voice streamed out, sounding confident, sure of herself, completely unlike the hunched, confused old woman in the booth.

"I... I remember that," she said slowly. "I remember seeing the box appear and fireworks blasting up the wall. Jocelyn and Nancy yelling and leaping away. But I also remember seeing Margay put it on the floor -- even though I don't remember seeing it before the explosion. Both those things can't be true."

"No, they can't."

Louise looked up at him. "Somebody put me under a spell. That was a Bard on the phone, wasn't it? Because why else would I have done what she said to do when the whole thing was crazy? I'd have to be stupid to come to something like this. I could have gotten hurt a lot worse than I did. Or ended up in jail if we hurt someone."

Her eyes widened in sudden horror. "Oh, God, I punched and *kicked* you! I'm so sorry! Why on earth would I have done something like that?"

"Like you said, you were under a spell. You wouldn't have done it otherwise."

She looked up at Jocelyn, who was wiping down the table in another booth. "Can I... Can I still have some of that tea? And maybe those cookies?" She swallowed as her eyes filled with tears.

"Of course you can, Louise." Jocelyn headed into the kitchen.

A tear rolled down the old woman's face. "What's happening to this town? Why would anyone do this?" She looked over at Margay's straight, slim back as she watched the street beyond. Standing guard. "Margay's always been a good girl. Her mama was so proud of her medals... Like I was proud of my Tom's from Vietnam."

Her gaze hardened, and her voice took on a fierce note. "When you serve, that means something. People shouldn't do you like we did her today." Another tear rolled down her face. "Maybe I do have Alzheimer's."

Nancy slid into the booth next to her and put an arm around her. "You don't have Alzheimer's. Some Bard bitch put a spell on you to get you here."

"But *why*? Why would anyone target Jocelyn and

Margay and the Spoon? Why would a Bard send us after you?"

That was a damned good question.

Chapter Nine

"It's not just a Bard," Grant said, and began to tick off incidents on his fingers. "It took an Arcanist to spell that box, and an alchemist to make whatever drug was *in* the box."

"The Bard could've bought the spell and the drug," Margay pointed out, turning at last. Cautiously, she walked over to join them, her gaze on Mrs. Jones.

The old woman shifted uneasily, but she met Margay's gaze steadily. "I'm not going to be afraid of you. I'm *not*."

Jocelyn walked in carrying a tray with a teapot, sugar, creamer, and several mugs. She put a dessert plate with a pair of Christmas cookies down in front of Mrs. Jones, along with the cup of tea. "Be careful with that, it's hot. It's just some chamomile."

The woman looked down at the food, hesitated, then picked up the cookie and took a bite. As she chewed, the tense determination on her face softened into nostalgia. "This tastes just like that little cake." Her lips quivered, then firmed.

Gently, Grant questioned her about any strangers she'd seen in the past twenty-four hours, but she didn't remember anyone.

"Where did that Bard get my number?" she asked suddenly. "My cell number isn't in the phone book. I've still got a land line, but she called on my cell."

"Did you give it to anyone?" Grant asked as sirens wailed in the distance -- the ambulance. He was running out of time…

Louise frowned as if searching her memory. "Well, there was that customer… She walked into

Shear Excellence right after you left."

Grant tensed as excitement stirred. "And you gave her your number? Can you describe the woman?"

Mrs. Jones paused in the act of taking a sip of her tea. "What woman?"

"The woman you saw in Shear Excellence."

"You mean the stylist? That was Elaine Bates. You know her -- she owns the shop."

Grant was beginning to wonder if she did have Alzheimer's after all. "You said there was a woman who came in the salon after I did."

The old woman frowned, opened her mouth, closed it again. She shook her head. "I don't... There wasn't a woman. I didn't see anyone but Elaine." She rubbed her temple. "God, my head... My head is killing me. Maybe I'm hurt worse than I thought."

Before he could question her again, the ambulance pulled up in front of the restaurant, and its siren cut off.

A moment later, Margay opened the door for the EMTs, who wheeled in a stretcher. She pointed out Louise, and the paramedics headed over.

While one of them took Mrs. Jones's blood pressure, Jocelyn told the other she'd given Louise a cookie and chamomile tea.

The tech gave her an unfriendly look. "You put anything else in it?"

Grant saw the moment Jocelyn's temper uncharacteristically snapped. "No, I didn't. I didn't even sacrifice a chicken or pray to Satan."

The tech smirked at her. "With an attitude like that, it's no wonder you're getting such shitty Yelp reviews."

Jocelyn said frostily, "We have four and a half stars over hundreds of reviews."

"Not anymore, you don't." He turned away to help his partner assist Louise onto the stretcher. They wheeled her out as Margay again held the door for them.

Jocelyn pulled her cell phone out of her apron pocket and thumbed the screen. She hissed in dismay.

Crap, what now?

Margay moved to look over her shoulder, her eyes widening.

Grant frowned. Ever since *Magical Kitchens*, The Spoon had racked up tourist visits and glowing reviews. Had somebody…

"Oh, hell, the Spoon's entire front page is nothing but one-star reviews!" Margay swore as her mother dropped into a booth seat.

"They trolled us," Jocelyn said numbly. "They spammed our reviews."

Grant winced. He'd heard of teams of Humanist trolls pulling that kind of crap targeting Talents before.

Jocelyn began to cry. "I've worked so hard. Everything I've done, all my hard work… All gone. In just a few hours."

Margay wrapped her arms around her mother. "God, Mama, I'm so sorry. I did this. I need to quit. They're after *me*. I'm going to have to leave town. Maybe if I'm not here…"

"No!" Jocelyn straightened as if jabbed with a pin and met her gaze fiercely despite the tears. "We can move to Laurelton. That's a Talent town. Heck, we can just *move*. They *like* Talents in New York."

"We couldn't afford the rent."

Grant swore silently as he watched the two women huddle together. Just when he was beginning to make progress with Margay, she'd decided to leave again.

Oh, hell no! He opened his mouth, but before he could say anything, Jocelyn smoothed a long curl back from her daughter's face. "None of this is about you, or even me. This is nothing but a bunch of people unhappy with their own lives. Abusing us makes them feel powerful." Her lip curled. "It's the bully M.O."

"Yeah, maybe, when it comes to the online trolls who don't even live here. But that crowd's anger was directed at *me*," Margay told her. "That MEED was aimed *at me* -- designed to trigger my PTSD. If I..."

Grant had heard about enough. "The Bard who's working with the Feral did this -- *not* you. Once we catch those creeps, the spell will wear off and people will forget all this."

Swiping impatiently at the tears in her eyes, Jocelyn said, "Maybe, but the fact is, this state is getting more and more unfriendly to Talents. But that isn't true everywhere. We can move. New York, Chicago, Seattle. Or New Orleans! I love New Orleans."

"Mama, you paid off the mortgage on this place. We can't throw away a fifty-year-old business and just start over somewhere else. Then you really would be starting from nothing."

"Not nothing," Jocelyn defended herself. "The *Magical Kitchens* thing gave me an audience. I might even be *more* successful somewhere else..."

Grant folded his arms. "What would Darrell think about Whitfields tucking tail and running?" Which was dirty pool, but the idea of them leaving filled him with too much desperation to pull his punches. "Leaving is a permanent solution to a temporary problem. I'd much rather catch these assholes -- however many of them there are -- than take the risk that they'll follow you wherever you go and do the same thing all over again."

Margay looked up at him, her eyes narrowing with temper. She didn't like him bringing up her father -- probably because he was right about Darrell's reaction. "Grant, they're targeting our mothers. Our. *Mothers.* Your mom could've been hurt too."

"So the solution is to leave me unemployed?" Nancy demanded, striding in from the kitchen.

"Better to lose your job than your life," Margay retorted.

"If we catch them it won't come to that," Grant said.

"We don't even know who *they* are."

Her mother looked up at her, and a muscle set in her jaw in an expression Grant recognized from his childhood. "Maybe you're right about giving this time to die down. We need to close the restaurant..." As Grant opened his mouth to protest, she lifted a hand at him. "Just for a week, maybe two. That will give you and Margay a chance to find out who's doing this. The Bard goes to jail, any spells wear off, and I can decide what to do about this mess."

While they'd been talking, Jocelyn's other employees had filtered into the dining room, attracted by the raised voices. Brenda Hollings, Shanna Price, and Joe Jeffries all wore matching worried expressions.

"But if you close the restaurant, even for a few days..." Joe shook his head. He was a tall, thin Black Alchemist with short, gray-flecked braids. "I wasn't planning on this. Jos, I need that money."

Jocelyn turned to him. "I realize that. Look, I've got money socked away in a rainy-day fund in case equipment breaks, and right now things are definitely broken." She gave her watching workers a tight smile. "Congratulations, you all get Christmas week off with pay. It's the least I can do, given the circumstances."

The staff visibly relaxed.

"But are you going to quit and move the restaurant?" Shanna demanded, looking anxious. "I'll follow you, but Felix is in first grade. I don't want to have to pull him out when he's finally making friends. You know how hard that is for a Talent kid."

Jocelyn sighed. She looked so exhausted -- she seemed to have aged twenty years. "I don't know. And yes, I realize all of your livelihoods would be affected, not just ours. But I want you out of the line of fire. I want us *all* out of the line of fire, but I can't control that. We'll just have to do the best we can." She looked around at the restaurant. "I think we've got everything cleaned up. You've got the rest of the day off. Merry Christmas."

But the three didn't look nearly as happy as you'd expect from people who'd just gotten a paid vacation. One by one they came over to hug their boss and Margay, murmuring encouragement.

The worry on all their faces sent a wash of hot anger through Grant. *I've got to find those Talent assholes and make them pay for this.*

As Joe, Shanna, and Brenda headed back into the kitchen to leave through the back door, Grant dropped a hand on Margay's shoulder and leaned in. "We need to talk. We've *got* to put our heads together and figure out what the hell is going on."

She turned to look up at him, and her lips trembled. "I can deal with these jerks. I've fought worse. But endangering Mama, Nancy, and you..." She shook her head wearily.

Grant ignored the fact he was still on duty and pulled her into a hug. But as they touched, the scent of her body flooded his senses. Desire sucker punched him, hot and ferocious, and to his horror, he realized he was getting an erection -- in front of their mothers.

Margay's golden eyes widened as she stared up at him, nostrils flaring as if sampling his scent. Raz rumbled, a deep sound that was somehow interested.

Nancy gave them a long look, then turned to Jocelyn and clapped her hands. "I think it's time for another ladies' night, Jos. We can go back to my place, watch the whole *Magic Mike* series and drink margaritas. I need a visit with Jose Cuervo."

Jocelyn eyed Margay and Grant, the grim set of her mouth easing. Then she looked at her friend and drawled in a bad Mathew McConaughey impression, "All right all right all right!"

Margay frowned. "I don't think that's such a good idea. I don't want that damn Feral showing up at your house the way he did at Grant's."

At that reminder, both women lost their grins. "Oh, hell," Nancy said. "I didn't think of that."

"Actually, I'd rather you get out of town completely. Maybe head to the beach or something, so Grant and I can concentrate on catching these guys."

The two mothers exchanged a look. "We can do that," Jocelyn said slowly.

"I put some money away for that trip to New Orleans we've been talking about," Nancy suggested.

"That would do it," Margay agreed.

"We'll need to book a round-trip flight and a hotel," Jocelyn said, and pulled out her phone. The two women slid into a booth and put their heads together over the device.

Grant turned to Margay. "I need to get back to the station. But since I don't have to work a patrol shift tonight, why don't you come over to my house at eight? I'll fix dinner and we can discuss this mess."

She looked up at him, and he saw a flash of heat

in her golden eyes. "Sounds good. I'll see you then." Margay caught his hand, the heat replaced by worry. "But be careful. If you hear so much as a growl, call me. Raz and I can be there in seconds."

He smiled back, though his male pride was stung. But since she was better equipped to fight a tiger than he was, he sucked it up. "I'll do that." Though seriously tempted to kiss her, Grant contented himself with a squeeze of her hand, then headed out the door.

* * *

Margay watched him leave, wishing he wasn't too damned professional for a kiss. God, she craved his touch until it was a physical ache. The thought that they'd be alone tonight sent a thrill of anticipation through her.

With a sigh, she got up to flip off the Spoon's neon OPEN light. "We'll need to put up a sign saying we'll be closed through New Year's."

Jocelyn looked up from her cell. "Mind printing that out?"

"Sure." She walked to the office that lay off the kitchen and got to work. Five minutes later, she was taping the message to the door. Margay winced. "I'm so damned sorry I got you into this."

"We've already had this conversation and I don't want it to turn into another fight," Jocelyn said, without looking around as Nancy scribbled notes on a pad. "Not. Your. Fault." To Nancy she added, "We can put that flight on my card. With the Christmas travel rush on, it's the best we're going to do."

As Margay winced in guilt, Raz manifested fully and padded over to rub her big head up and down against Jocelyn's shoulder. Knowing big cat habits from years of living with Darrell's, Mama gave the glowing tiger a good scratch under the chin. Margay felt the ghostly echo of it under her own jaw.

"You're a good kitty," Mama said to Raz in the high singsong people used with pets. It sounded more than a little odd addressed to three hundred pounds of magical killing machine. "I wish you'd go eat yourself a mean old Bard, maybe have an Arcanist creep for dessert. Yes, I do, you big ol' puss."

"And I'd love to do it -- if we can find the bastard," Margay told her. "Or bastards."

Jocelyn slanted her a look past the tiger's great glowing head. "Margay, language."

Margay jutted a thumb at her own chest. "Mom, Arcane Corps."

Her mother huffed. "Yes, Arcane Corps -- *not* the Navy. You're not a sailor and I don't want you swearing like one."

Margay laughed and slid into the booth across from the two women.

"You and Grant seem to be getting along," Nancy observed, sounding a little sly.

"Yeah, but…" She shook her head. "It creates a serious conflict of interest."

Nancy snorted. "Dear, he doesn't *care*. He's always been in love with you. I figured you two would get hitched right out of high school."

"Instead, he married someone else," Margay said, a trifle bitterly.

"He told me before the wedding he didn't think you were interested in him anymore because he was a normie."

"No, it was because I was a Tooth Tank, and when I'm manifested, I'm three times as strong as he is. That's the kind of thing that turns guys off. Even Austin --"

"Austin was no loss," Jocelyn interrupted. "I had my fingers crossed you weren't going to end up with that jerk. I've seen that kind of toxic snake make life hell for my waitresses. Austin might have more education than most of them -- *and* a tiger -- but he's still the same species of prick."

Margay grinned. "Language."

Her mother stuck her tongue out at her, and she laughed.

* * *

That night, Margay drove to Grant's rental. She hadn't really looked at the place the last time she'd been here -- she'd been too afraid the enemy tiger was going to kill him.

The house was a long one-story brick ranch of the type that was everywhere in the south. It looked as if it dated back to the 1970s, with its black shutters and a door set with a brass knocker. Azaleas and holly bushes clustered out front, along with a pair of spindly dogwoods that were probably lovely in the spring.

Margay parked behind Grant's Ford Interceptor and the blue Toyota Camry that was his personal vehicle. She slid out of her own Honda, then gave her skirt a tug. She'd wanted to dress up for him, so she'd put on a red silk dress with a handkerchief hem that was short and deliberately sexy, with crimson high heels and careful makeup.

Her mother, meanwhile, had insisted on making the cake she knew was Grant's favorite before she and Nancy drove off to Charlotte to catch their flight to New Orleans.

When Grant opened the door, Margay's eyes widened. He was dressed in a black shirt and slacks that made him look like distilled sex. She had the satisfaction of watching a wicked, admiring smile bloom across his face at the sight of her. "I see you brought dessert," he purred, sounding like a big cat himself.

She grinned and handed him the cake carrier. "Yep."

"I wasn't talking about the cake." Holding the carrier aside, he leaned in and took her mouth with a slow, seductive slide of lips and tongue. She kissed him back, savoring the feeling of his cock hardening against her as heat flashed the length of her body from lips to heels.

When he finally drew away, they were both breathing hard. "I'd better put this cake on the kitchen counter before I drop it," he murmured. "My entire blood supply seems to be heading south."

Margay grinned back. "I noticed."

"I'd certainly hope so." Grant turned and led the way. As they passed into the living room, she took a good look around.

It was a thoroughly masculine space. The sofa and armchairs were upholstered in brown distressed leather trimmed with studded brass nail heads. A small Christmas cedar, live and fragrant, stood in one corner, decorated with blue and silver ornaments and winding silver tinsel.

Grant always had loved Christmas.

Floor-to-ceiling bookshelves lined the walls, crammed with books -- tomes on forensics, interrogation, serial killers, magical crimes -- and dog-eared science fiction paperbacks, some of which she recognized from their childhood.

But what drew her eye was the shelf that held a familiar figurine she'd given him the Christmas of their senior year. She wandered over for a closer look.

Batman stood with his arms around Catwoman, who had a whip wrapped around his throat and a wicked, satisfied smile on her pretty face.

Batman looked horny.

Margay chuckled. "I did not realize how kinky this thing was when I bought it for you. And I can't believe you're displaying it now. Kind of cuts against the whole *dead serious law enforcement professional* thing you've got going in the rest of the decor."

Grant gave her a long, sensual stare. "I don't give a damn -- you gave it to me. Every time I'd look at it, I'd dream of being with a certain cat woman of my very own." He hooked her in with his free hand for another kiss, even more slow and thorough than the last. Cupping her breast through the thin silk of her dress, he brushed his thumb over the pebbled peak. The long, brash length of him nudged her belly, insistent behind the expensive fabric of his slacks.

But just as he started to drag her even closer, something buzzed from the next room. He groaned and let her go. "That's the timer. I've got to get the lasagna out of the oven." He flashed her a grin. "Mom's recipe."

Her eyebrows flew up. His mother was a damn good cook, and her lasagna was a favorite of Margay's. Jocelyn always said that dish didn't need magic -- it had it already. And she wasn't just flattering Nancy either.

The kitchen was as minimalist as you'd expect in a bachelor rental -- a fridge, a Keurig coffee maker, an elderly stove, a microwave and a dishwasher. A small round table occupied the breakfast nook, draped in a lace tablecloth, with a pair of lit candles in silver candlesticks flanking a poinsettia arrangement. He'd set the table with pretty china plates, flatware, and crystal wine glasses.

He really did go all out. What does he have in mind? No, scratch that -- she knew what he had in mind. Mostly because she was thinking the same thing.

Raz chuffed, evidently approving.

Her attention fell on the salad sitting ready on the counter. Not just a store-bought blend of iceberg lettuce and shredded carrots, either -- he'd put what looked like most of a vegetable garden in there, topped off with the raspberry vinaigrette Jocelyn sold.

Grant put the cake carrier down beside the salad, then went to get the lasagna out of the oven.

While the dish rested, he poured a couple of glasses of red wine and handed one to Margay. As they sipped it, their eyes met. His were hot and hooded, and every time his lips touched his glass, Margay felt the slow, liquid rise of warmth between her thighs.

Sex was so thick in the room, you could have cut it like the cake.

Finally they plated the lasagna and salad, along with the crusty French bread he'd prepared, and sat down to eat. Margay was acutely conscious of every move he made -- his mouth closing around each bite, the grace of his big, capable hands. The way he watched her more often than he looked at his food.

"You ever get the feeling our mothers are trying to matchmake?" he asked, his voice sounding deeper than usual, his southern accent blurring the consonants into a low rumble.

"Absolutely." Margay smiled at him over the lip of her wine glass. "That whole bit about *Magic Mike* was flat-out blatant. They wanted us to know we'd have the apartment to ourselves."

"They didn't really have to work that hard at it," he told her, his lids dipping over eyes gone dark in the candlelight. "I've never stopped loving you."

"Yeah, I could tell by the way you got married." The minute the words were out of her mouth, Margay winced and put her glass down. "This wine is maybe just a little bit too good."

"*In vino veritas*." He studied her. "Is that the reason you've been avoiding me?"

She played with her fork. "Maybe one of them."

Grant nodded slowly, and silence fell again. She forked up more of the lasagna, barely tasting it for the tension, sexual and otherwise.

"When I went to work for the Laurelton Sheriff's Office," he said at last, "my field training officer was an older deputy, John Clayton -- he's retired now. He's a Melded lion Feral, fought in the first Gulf War. His wife, Georgia, is an Arcanist. I spent weeks riding around in his patrol car while he taught me the ins and outs of law enforcement. John and Georgia more or less adopted me. Kind of like your mom and dad."

His expression lightened, his gaze turning inward. "They have a real bond. Loved each other like nobody I've ever seen, except for your folks. They could almost read each other's minds."

"Yeah, Mama always swore Dad was as empathetic with her as his cat."

"Darrell Whitfield was empathic with everybody." He took a bite of his lasagna, chewed. Swallowed. "I saw Georgia cast Arc spells a few times. Sometimes John would close his eyes and just watch with this wondering smile on his face, like she was the most amazing thing he'd ever seen. Of course, when I closed mine, I didn't see anything, since I have all the Talent of a pinecone."

Margay eyed him, wondering where he was going with this. Decided to try a joke, in part to make up for the nasty crack about his marriage. "You have plenty of talent -- it's just not for magic."

He ignored that, intent on whatever point he had in mind. "One night I had to break up a fight at this bar and took a bottle upside the head. Ended up going to the ER. Brandy was the nurse who patched me up. She started flirting, let me know she was single. Liked the way I looked. I was polite, but that's about it."

Margay's hand tightened on her fork. She looked down to find claws glowing softly on her fingertips. Willed them to vanish.

Grant didn't seem to notice. "When I got home, I checked my email, hoping for something from you. There was nothing -- hadn't been anything in a while. Your mother told me later you were up in the Hindu Kush -- didn't have Internet access. Anyway, that's when it hit me that you were out there with other people, other Talents. People who could close their eyes and see magic. And it occurred to me that if you could find an Arcanist -- a male version of John's wife -- he'd be better for you than I would."

Irritation stung her, rendered even more intense because she could understand how he'd feel that way. "And it never occurred to you to just *ask*?"

"Yeah, that was stupid," Grant admitted, and sighed. "But then I had to take a guy to the ER because his heart was acting up. A foot chase and enough meth will do that. Anyway, there was Brandy, flirting. And I… ended up asking her out. You and me…" He shook his head. "I thought there was no way we'd ever work."

We could have. You just didn't give us a chance. She managed to keep her mouth shut only with intense effort.

"Brandy had a way of making me feel like… I

was her hero." He grimaced. "What a dumbass reason to marry someone. We never really loved one another. We were just tired of being alone."

So was I, Margay thought.

"I did try to love her." His lip curled. "At least until I found out she was doing half the cops in the department to get back at me. She'd twigged to the fact I was still in love with you. Apparently, I talked about you a little bit too much." He rolled his eyes. "Okay, a *lot* too much."

And right now, I know just how she felt. I really shouldn't have opened this can of worms. "For the record, I don't give a damn about whether you have magic or not," Margay told him, working hard to keep her voice from rising. "I *had* a partner with magic, and I found out real damn quick magic doesn't make up for more important things. What matters is the connection -- the *love*. Making love to you when we were teenagers was incredible, even though neither one of us knew what the hell we were doing. You were -- and *are* -- a far better lover than Austin, despite his experience. Because unlike him, you care enough to work at it. Your focus is always on me instead of yourself."

"Because yours is on *me*," Grant said, and took a deep swallow of his wine. "I should have trusted you instead of listening to my own insecurity."

"Yeah, you really should have."

"Point is, I want to be with *you*, Margay." He put the glass down and reached out to wrap one big, warm hand around hers. His gaze was open, vulnerable. "I never stopped loving you, even when I thought I should."

"And I never stopped loving you. Never stopped *wanting* you. We've got a bond that doesn't need magic." Then she sighed. "But right now, I constitute a huge conflict of interest for you. I know the mayor -- Sean Miller has his eye on running for the South Carolina House next year. If he thinks you're a political liability, he'll fire you."

Grant scowled, his jaw taking on a stubborn jut. "Then I'll get a job somewhere else."

"Not if there's a scandal."

"But there won't *be* one if we can solve this thing." He leaned in, his gaze intent. "Margay, what happened to Raz? Because my gut tells me this all goes back to that bomb."

Margay rose from the table, but his gaze stayed locked on her face. Listening to him talk about Brandy had given her a hot need to remind him just what they had. That it was *real*.

She circled the table and leaned down, deliberately giving him a good view down her cleavage. "I'm not in the mood to talk about the bomb. You never finished showing me the house. And I want to see your bedroom."

For a moment, he didn't move, looking up at her. Weighing. At last his lips curled into a slow, hot smile, and he rose to his feet to take her hand. "Then by all means, let's finish the tour."

Chapter Ten

Grant obviously had seduction in mind, judging from his bedroom. Clusters of unlit votive candles stood on the bureau and chest of drawers, not to mention the nightstands that flanked his king-size bed.

The furniture itself was simple oak, with clean, square lines. The comforter was covered in big, asymmetrical blocks of navy blue and slate gray.

But what caught her attention was the bureau, where two pictures stood in matching silver frames. Walking over, she saw one was a photo of the two of them at their senior prom. Grant looked lean and handsome in a black tux, the promise of the man evident in the boy. Margay wore a slim gold sheath that made her eyes look bright with boundless optimism. No sign of the ghosts her mirror showed now.

Next to that stood a photo of herself in her Arcane Corps body armor, kneeling with one arm draped across Razia's furry belly, as the tigress sprawled across her lap on her back, paws dangling in the air like a giant house cat. It had been taken when she and Raz were still on their first tour. Margay had been so ridiculously proud of being assigned a tiger, she grinned like a pumpkin. "Look at that little idiot. Thinks she's twelve feet tall and bulletproof."

Grant lifted a brow. "Weren't you?"

"Only on paper." Before the Marine convoy attack, the girls' school, and way too many Caliphate Ferals who'd done their best to kill her.

And then there'd been Ukraine…

…the MEED was right there, right in front of her, and the air stank with the petroleum reek of RDX and rang

with Czar's terrified roar…

"Margay?" Strong arms encircled her waist, and she jolted back to the present as Grant turned her to face him. "You okay, baby?"

"Fine," she lied, and forced a smile.

He gave her a long, level look. "No. You're not. Don't lie to me, Margay. I can't help you if you lie -- to me or yourself."

"Some days a good lie is all that keeps me sane."

But as she looked at him, she thought of a much better way to exorcize her many, many ghosts. Stepping full against him, she grabbed a fistful of his shirt, and pulled him in for a hot, open-mouthed kiss. He froze for a moment as if unsure whether to let her change the subject. Margay pulled back a fraction and breathed, "Please…"

He didn't deny her. With a sound halfway between a growl and a moan, he went in for a kiss of his own, slow, gentle, as his hands slid around her waist and drew her in. Let her feel his cock going hard against her.

Hunger slammed into Margay, sweeping away the pain and fear as Raz made the air around them vibrate in a hungry rumble.

He drew back a little, and his passion-flushed lips curled in a slow smile. "Was that you or Raz?"

"Both. God, both." Margay swayed into him, stretching up to meet his mouth, relishing the warm contours of his muscular body. "I just… just don't want to think. Don't want to remember."

"I'll see what I can do." Parted lips found hers again, and she opened her own for the ravenous sweep of his tongue. He made a little growling sound as he slipped inside her mouth, swirling and licking, tasting of wine and lasagna. One hand slid to her ass, fingers tracing swirling patterns over the thin fabric of her short skirt. Found the crease between her cheeks, traced a forefinger down it, then slipped down to slide beneath the skirt. Feathered swirling patterns over the skin on his way to the waistband of her panties. Slid beneath, cupping her ass from behind.

His hand was big enough to palm her as it slid down, following the curve of her ass. Breath growing rough, she rolled her hips back and up at his hand.

Grant took that for the invitation it was, two fingers gliding to cup her inner lips from behind. Began scissoring them apart and together, massaging her pussy between them. She felt herself growing as wet as he was hard.

And every breath she drew with her cat-enhanced senses carried the taste of Grant's arousal. She moaned into his mouth. He tilted her chin up so he could nuzzle along the length of her jaw, paused to blow a warm gust along her ear. Leaned in for a lick and nibble at her earlobe that made her shiver at the sensation.

Suddenly he pulled back, gave her a wicked little grin. "Hold that thought," he murmured. "I've got an idea…"

With that, he turned and…

…Left the room.

Margay stared after him, her eyebrows flying up even as Raz gave a frustrated little chuff. *Planning to surprise me? Think I'll return the favor…*

* * *

Five minutes later Grant was back, only to find the bedroom door closed. His heart sank. Apparently, his little brainstorm had been a bad idea. *She's pissed.*

This was the kind of thing Brandy used to do --

getting him stirred up only to close the door in his face.

With Brandy, that kind of shit had barely stung. But this was Margay, and he felt a little sick. He cleared his throat and called through the door, "I brought wine and cake." *Please don't lock me out.*

"What are you waiting for?" she called, Raz rumbling an echo. "Come on in."

He relaxed. Well, she didn't *sound* pissed. And come to think of it, Margay had never played Brandy's kind of games anyway. Grant propped the tray with his offerings against his hip and used his free hand to open the door. Stepped inside.

And froze.

Margay stood at the bureau, gloriously naked except for crimson stilettos and black thigh-high stockings with a line of red rosebud appliqués up the side of each glorious leg. She'd found the butane lighter he'd bought and was just lighting the last of the white votives he'd set up on the dresser for his planned seduction. When she looked around at him, candlelight painted the side of her face and reflected in her Feral gold eyes.

More of the votives scattered around the room poured soft yellow light over her body with its long, deliciously erotic curves. "Come on in," she said, her voice low and seductive as any Bard's.

Grant went from cold and sick to rock-hard in three heartbeats. "I thought we could have dessert," he said, his own voice low and rough as he shut the door behind him.

Her brilliant gaze dipped below his belt. "You do look hungry."

"Oh, you have no idea." He walked toward her, hardening with every step, to slide the tray onto the bureau beside the candles. The wine glasses chimed against one another -- he'd done it a little too hard.

As he steadied the tray, she stepped against his side until her breath heated his skin under the thin fabric of his shirt. She leaned in and bit the line of his jaw, barely hard enough to sting.

He turned and reached for her, but she danced away and strolled to the bed, that perfect ass of hers rolling with every step on those wicked stilettos.

Reaching the bed, she bent one long leg to pull off a scarlet high heel. Staring at the lush curves of her tempting ass, he felt saliva flood his mouth, balls tightening as his cock pressed painfully against his fly. She put her stocking-clad foot down and dropped the shoe with a little *thunk* on the hardwood floor. Bending the other knee, she twisted to tug off that shoe even more slooooowly. Candlelight painted warm brown skin, gleaming on curves and hollows and the slide of lean muscle. The other heel went *thunk*.

Oh, sweet God. He'd never wanted a woman more in his life. Grant moved closer, half-hypnotized by the sleek sensuality of the movement as she bent, picked up the heels, and put them neatly aside. Each gesture displayed that gorgeous body, so long and perfect.

Then she climbed up on the bed with its soft, puffy comforter and crawled toward the pillow. Mouth dry, Grant stared at the working swells of her lovely glutes.

It was his turn to growl.

Margay turned and settled back into the pillows piled against the oak headboard and lifted a challenging brow. She picked up a few of her long braids and brushed them over one hard, dark nipple. "Your turn," she told him. "Put on a show."

That stopped him in his tracks. "What?"

"You heard me." She turned to the nightstand

beside the bed and picked up her cell phone, did something on the screen. Raven's lush voice poured out of the phone, singing "You're Pure Magic," the music of guitar, piano and drums slow, as darkly seductive as Margay's long, long legs. "Show me all the magic." She lifted a dark brow, brushing the braids back and forth over one tight brown nipple. "And don't say you don't have any, because that's a damn lie."

"Is it?" Hesitating, Grant recalibrated, then started toward her, stepping in rhythm with the Bard's powerful voice. He was no Primo, but Margay had taught him how to dance before they'd hit puberty. As he walked, he began to unbutton his shirt, one button at a time. Opening a V of skin, watching with satisfaction as her gold gaze dropped to watch. "Because next to you…"

"Don't sell yourself short. That's a really *outstanding* wand." Her mouth curled in a witchy grin, before the smile faded, lips softening. Voice low, she said, "Nobody else has ever touched me like you do. That's why I've never been able to want anybody else. Not even when I thought I'd lost you."

"You could never lose me." He pulled his shirt out of his waistband. "Not since I was a skinny, hungry, lonely little kid who hadn't eaten in two days after Dad cleaned out our bank account." He smiled, remembering. "You took me back into the Spoon's kitchen while Mom filled out that job application. Then you fixed me a plate with more food than I'd seen in a month and told me you'd be my friend." He paused, his gaze nakedly vulnerable. "I wanted the friend even more than the food."

"I didn't have anybody either. Not until you." She licked her lips and leaned back against the pile of pillows, sliding those long, long legs apart, giving him an excellent view of the dark curls between them. "After you, there was never anybody else. You were all the magic I needed."

He stopped in front of the bed to pull off the black shirt, rolling his shoulders, his hips, spreading his feet wide. His pants were slowly strangling his dick, but he ignored that ache as he slid the shirt down the length of his arms, exaggerating the twist and roll undressing called for. Dropped the shirt to pool around his feet.

Her gold eyes looked a little glazed, and Razia rumbled, the sound a deep, hungry thrum that might have been sinister under any other circumstances.

Instead, it made him grin.

* * *

Grant could have danced Channing Tatum right off the stage, despite the actor's Primo Talent. His green eyes on hers, he folded his arms behind his head, making those thick biceps bunch as he rolled his hips. Muscle worked along his wide torso with its dusting of dark hair -- seductive ripples she ached to touch, to taste.

Just as maddening, a thin treasure trail of hair led down to a bulge in his slacks that could have put a Clydesdale to shame. She remembered how that luscious cock had felt when they'd made love -- the deep, driving thrusts, the blaze of shattering pleasure. The feel of his mouth on her clit, his teeth nibbling delicately, driving her half-crazy.

It was all she could do not to tackle him and ride him to the floor.

Instead, she met his sensual gaze, one hand busy with her own nipple, the other sliding the length of her body to stroke through her pussy hair. Watching his eyes lock on her fingers. Returning his show with her own.

He toed off his dress shoes, then ran a hand down to his fly. Unfastened a button, a hook. Unzipped his slacks. His cock jutted hungrily, barely contained by the black cotton of his boxers. He hooked the waistband of his pants and boxers with his thumbs and bent slooooowly, working them down the length of his legs. Bending double as he stripped his pants off, giving her a mouth-watering view of his bent back. He paused long enough to shed his socks, then straightened again. The long shaft of his cock bounced a little with the movement, and he paused there, his body rolling with the music as he stared at her.

RRrrrmmmmm, Razia rumbled, reacting to Margay's hunger. As she panted like an overheated cat, Grant's scent teased her. There was his unique fragrance, but overlaying that was the musk of lust -- and something else, something sweeter, something she'd never smelled in another man.

She'd never known love had a scent before.

As Margay watched, a clear drop of pre-cum formed on the tip of his cock. And she was feeling pretty wet herself. She slid off the bed and went to him, rolling her own hips to the music. He rolled his hips right back, his cock giving an impudent bounce…

So she grabbed it, wrapping her long fingers tight around the thick shaft, giving him a long, slow tug. His eyes almost crossed. "Holy God, Margay…"

"Mmm…" She purred back and started to drop to her knees. *This calls for a blowjob…*

"Nope," he said, grabbing her around the waist and arresting her drop, hauling her upward into his arms instead. She wrapped her legs around his lean waist and hooked her feet together as she hugged his strong neck.

For a moment they just stared at one another in the candlelight. His eyes looked all pupil, black with arousal, his lips flushed and parted as he breathed hard, almost panting from teasing and being teased.

His cock pressed hard against her belly, temptingly close to where she most wanted him. *Thick and hard, and Oh, God, I'm not going to be able to hold off long...*

So she gave him her best cheeky grin and leaned in to taste his mouth, slow and tender, even as she rolled her hips against that impressive erection. "Want a piece of me, white boy?"

"God, yes," he rumbled, and closed his teeth gently over her lower lip for a slow nibble, then tightening his mouth for a nursing suckle. All the while he rolled his hips, teasing her with the promise of that meaty prick.

Deciding she'd had about as much as she could take, Margay tightened the grip of her locked ankles and lifted herself with her thighs, freeing one hand from his neck. But before she could reach between her legs and aim him properly, he said, "Nope. And anyway, we need a condom."

He bent over the bed to put her down, bracing himself with one hand on the mattress. Margay considered several wicked possibilities that would turn the tables, but before she could settle on one, he pulled away and headed to the nightstand.

He fished around in a drawer until he came out with a condom. Lazily, she watched him start pulling it on. Mostly to drive him nuts, she slid a hand between her thighs and started tracing circles over her clit.

His eyes widened and glazed as they locked on

her busy fingers.

Raz chuffed as she started teasing one nipple with her free hand, squeezing, tugging. His cock bucked upward, and she licked her lips, remembering the way it tasted, the way it filled her mouth, her pussy…

Deliberately, she bent one knee up, then straightened it into the air, pointing her toes at the ceiling. Raised the other leg to rub her thighs together, trapping her hand against her pussy. Enjoying the added pressure on her clit.

"Jesus God, Margay…" he growled, and dragged the condom on fast enough to make his cock dance.

Sheathed, he stepped over to the foot of the bed, grabbed her knees in both hands, lifted her butt off the mattress. She slapped her arms down, bracing her weight in a Yoga plank as he held her at an angle and speared hard into her cunt.

The sudden entry -- the feel of all that hard cock sliding so deep -- yanked a startled yelp out of her. *God, it feels so gooood*!

Raz chuffed and rumbled as Grant held her in position, the biceps of his arms bulging as he fucked and dug and ground.

Margay arched her back and shoved hard into him, meeting him thrust for thrust. Loving the way he arched back a little, the better to give her clit the perfect friction and stroke little knots of pleasure she hadn't even known she had. The tension gathered and gathered into a hard, pulsing ball of delight, winding the sweet spring of the building orgasm like a windlass.

Until it suddenly burst free, spitting fire up her spine, making her convulse and shake and yowl. Grant rammed to the balls, his head thrown back, his magnificent body painted in candlelight, roaring as he came.

Raz roared hard enough to shake the bed.

*   *   *

For a long, long moment they froze there, breath huffing, before Grant finally collapsed on the mattress beside her, panting. It took them a good five minutes to gather strength and breath enough to crawl to the pile of pillows by the headboard and collapse there. He flopped onto his back, then reached over and pulled her on top of him. She wrapped her arms around him and just dissolved into a boneless pile of smug, sated female.

Completely wrung out, she fell onto a happy doze, only dimly aware of his fingers tracing absent patterns on her shoulder.

"Margay," he said at last, and something in his tone made her eyes open. As she gave him a wary look, he said, "This Feral that targeted me -- I wasn't the target. Not the main target, anyway. That was you."

Damn it, can't he let it go for an hour? Maybe two?

No, he can't, retorted the more responsible part of her brain. *And neither can I. People's lives are at risk here. Including his.*

"The whole thing reminds me way too much of some of the uglier domestic cases I've worked," Grant continued. "Usually with an investigation like this, I start asking about husbands, lovers or exes. It's got that kind of intimate, nasty smell to it. This guy *knows* you -- knows the best way to hurt you. That's why he put that box behind the counter and lured your mom to the phone. He knew the fireworks alone wouldn't be enough to *really* trigger you, but your mama's scream-- that would do it. Anybody who *didn't* know you would have put the box out in the middle of the restaurant. It might've set you off, but pulling your mother into it..." He shook his head. "Yeah, he knows you. Knows how to wind you up. But if you are the main target, why not just shoot you?"

"Bulletproof, remember?"

"Only if you can get your manifestation up in time. He could easily have shot you with a scoped rifle on one of those midnight runs of yours. Or, for that matter, walking in and out of the restaurant." He fell silent, drumming his fingertips on her bare shoulders, thinking. "But you're not the only target. Somebody sent that video to the television stations. They wanted the Humanists stirred up."

"Yeah, that did seem designed to go viral," Margay said, frowning. "But why would Talents try to set the Humanists off? Every one of us is acutely aware we're balanced on a knife edge right now. Me going nuts in a restaurant and killing people would be enough to push us all off."

"Could be a situation like the Arcane Island case, or the Victoria Laurel thing. Rich conservatives hiring Talent assassins to do a little outrage farming." He considered that for a few minutes, then slowly shook his dark head. "No, still seems too personal. In the Victoria Laurel case, the assassin didn't start aiming attacks at Eva and Jake until the cops foiled a couple of their plans. But this was targeted directly at you from the start. I'd bet my badge it's a boyfriend."

She grinned at him. "The only boyfriend I have is you."

Grant lifted a dark brow. "What about Austin?"

She shook her head. "Can't be. He's the one who broke it off between us. And it was never love -- not even a reasonable facsimile. We were at best fuck buddies, and not even that when he started doing that Bard." Her head gave a warning throb, then began to pulse. She rubbed her temple, wincing. *So much for the lovely afterglow.*

Grant lifted his head and stared at her. "There was a Bard? And you didn't mention that before?"

"That was..." She bit off the words in Ukraine and substituted "... Overseas."

"So Ukraine."

Margay eyed him, irritated that he wouldn't let it go. God, her head was suddenly killing her. *I need some PowerUp.* "No."

He snorted. "So, what can you tell me about the bomb that killed Raz? Because I know you weren't in the Middle East when that happened. We've been out of there for years now. Somehow I don't see the Caliphate allowing their Bards to date American Corpsmen."

She frowned at him, wondering what the hell he was talking about. "Bards?"

"You just said you thought your ex was dating a Bard."

THROB. Damn, it was hard to think. Felt just like a backlash headache, which was weird, since she hadn't done any magic. "No, I didn't."

He blinked, as if startled, then his gaze sharpened. "You just said you thought Austin was doing a Bard."

"No, he took me to *see* a Bard."

"When was that?"

"The day before the bombing." She wished he'd shut up. She badly wanted to close her aching eyes and just sleep. She hadn't slept -- really *slept* -- in days now.

Grant stared at her for a long moment, and she had no idea what was bothering him. His gaze had taken on an edge. She had a sudden uncomfortable insight about what it must've been like to face Detective Grant Sawyer in an interview room. But she couldn't for the life of her imagine what she'd said to earn that look. Not with her head aching like a sore tooth.

Grant rolled over and lifted his cell phone from its charging cradle. "Why don't you tell me whatever you can about the bombing."

She eyed his phone. "Not if you're going to record it. I have no desire to end up in Leavenworth."

He promptly put the phone down again and told her gently, "I'm not trying to trap you. I'd sooner cut off my own arm."

Margay sighed. "I know. It's just… my head is *killing* me."

He studied her, then nodded. "Okay. I'll go get you a PowerUp."

She looked up at that, smiling a little. "Why do you have PowerUp?"

"Hoping I'd get lucky." He winked, then rolled from the bed and sauntered out stark naked.

He was back a few minutes later and handed her a bottle. As she downed it, Grant slid back into bed with her. He pulled her into his arms and stroked her hair quietly. The headache began to ease.

She really didn't want to talk about the bombing -- even thinking about it could bring on a flashback -- but he was right that he might spot something she didn't. A traumatic event didn't make for objectivity. "So ask your questions."

"Tell me whatever you can about the day of the bombing. You don't have to tell me where it was. Just what happened."

Margay fell silent, figuring out what to say and

how to say it. "We were training some… allies. Putting together a team of bonded Ferals, selecting the ones with the most power and potential. We'd whittled the group down to about thirty -- that was the number of Familiars we had."

"So these were little cubs? My Feral buddy Jake says y'all start training your Familiars when they're just a few weeks old."

"No, the timetable was too short for the way we do it in the US. They need to field fully bonded Feral teams now, not in a couple of years. It didn't matter if the bond wasn't quite as tight. These animals were a couple of years old. Not quite adults, but close."

"Same thing we did during World War II."

"Exactly. All the Familiars were in this enclosure -- a set of cages in a heavily fortified underground bunker. I was working on paperwork in my office when Raz started freaking the hell out. She just appeared in my head, absolutely frantic. And I knew something was really wrong."

"Smart cat."

"Oh, definitely. So I went down to the Familiar enclosures. I could hear the roars before I even got there. Every one of those animals was losing its mind -- bears, lions, tigers -- all of them just nuts. And the recruits were no better off. They weren't bonded to their animals yet, but Ferals are all animal empaths, so they could feel their Familiars' fear. So they were all trying to calm the critters down with their magic. That much noise is just not a good idea when there's a…" Margay remembered she was talking to a civilian and shut her mouth. Grant just raised an eyebrow in an *I'm not an idiot* expression. "But what really got my attention was Czar…"

"Czar?"

"Austin's tiger. He was pacing back and forth in his enclosure. Roaring, really agitated. I reached out to him..." Margay shook her head, remembering the chaos of the cat's mind. "Czar was a six-hundred-pound Amur tiger, and I'd never seen him frightened of anything. Pissed off, yeah -- Czar had an ugly temper. He didn't *do* terror, yet he was absolutely frantic. The other animals, including Raz, were all picking up on his anxiety, and it had set them all off."

Restlessly, she rolled out of bed and began to pace. There was no way she could tell the story sitting down.

"I figured there had to be a reason Czar was freaking. I scanned the area looking for magic -- maybe a bomb -- but there was no sign of anything. No booby traps, no fireworks, no nothing. So I called Austin's sat phone, since nobody else would be able to calm that animal down. Didn't get an answer. Texted him. Still no answer. I figured either he was off with his girlfriend, whoever the hell that was, or he was somewhere on base. I told the recruits to keep trying to calm their animals down and I'd go get Austin."

She pivoted to pace the other way, gathering her braids in her hands absently, petting them to soothe herself. "I headed for the Officers' Club because I figured that's where he'd be. I was about three blocks away from the bunker when Raz screamed in my head. Just this blast of absolute panic. And she showed me what she saw. There in the middle of the aisle between the cages was a MEED."

"But you looked for MEEDs." Grant watched her intently, eyes tracking her as she paced. "You said there was nothing there."

"Evidently the fucker that planted it slipped in right after I left. Judging by the patterns of magic, it was about to go off. There wasn't even time to run back. I projected my consciousness into Raz -- my body just toppled to the sidewalk. I'm lucky I didn't give myself a concussion. Instead of forming my cat, we manifested as a shell around the MEED. Just a sphere about a foot across, solid magic. We got the mani up about ten seconds before the MEED started going off."

* * *

Grant stared at her, watching her go pale despite her complexion, her golden eyes wide and unseeing. "We had to contain the explosion because the recruits were *right there, the animals were right there.* That blast would've killed all of them -- the whole unit wiped out.

"Raz and I poured everything we had into reinforcing the manifestation, building it as thick as we possibly could in the milliseconds we had. Our joined consciousness was *in* that manifestation -- that's what you have to do to make something that strong. I could feel the bomb going off. It couldn't have been more than a millisecond, but it seemed like forever. All this heat and energy, blowing us apart. I fought to hold it in because I knew the longer we contained it, the more recruits and Familiars we could save." She stopped in the middle of the room, eyes wide, staring at something thousands of miles away. "We held it and held it and its magic *burned* us... We might've been able to hold a hand grenade, but this was designed to take out the whole bunker and we just didn't have enough power." Tears ran in silver trails down her face. She didn't seem aware of them.

"Our mani finally exploded, and the MEED blasted shrapnel all around us. Raz and Czar were killed. Some of the other animals were burned or took shrapnel, but our cats were the only ones who died. We'd absorbed that much of it, anyway. The shock of all that energy, all that magic blasting us damn near finished Raz and me off, but somehow we ended up melded in my body. My heart stopped, but this Ukrainian soldier did CPR until the medics arrived."

"Jesus," Grant murmured, feeling sick at the thought of how close the bastards came to killing her.

"It took me hours to regain consciousness, and when I did, I didn't remember much. Memories came back only gradually. The doctors said it was some kind of magical shock from what we did. They did a CT scan and found I'd almost given myself a stroke. They tried to keep me in the service, but I started having flashbacks from the PTSD…" She shrugged. "Medical discharge."

"It sounds to me," he said slowly, "like Czar knew what was going to happen."

Margay stared at him as if the thought had never occurred to her. "Austin would've had to be involved. So, no."

"Are you sure? Where *was* Austin?" Grant asked.

Margay shrugged. "At this little restaurant he'd been frequenting. The Corps investigators questioned him about that, but witnesses said he was there the whole time."

Yeah, Grant wasn't buying that. *Time to try to get at the Bard thing again. See what she says.* "Was this the same restaurant where he took you to see the Bard?"

"Yeah. I was a little surprised he asked me out, to be honest. It hadn't been a pretty breakup. I figured he'd probably had a fight with his girlfriend, and was looking to hook up again, so at first I refused. But he said that the situation with the recruits was gonna be heating up soon. We really needed to bury the hatchet.

"So we went out. The food was okay, at best, but there was this Bard there." Her eyes went dreamy. "She had the most incredible voice. Kind of reminded me of Raven's back in the day. That kind of incredible range."

He had to be careful with this next bit. "Did you enjoy meeting her?"

"Yeah. We went back to her dressing room after the show, and I told her she needed to come to the States. That she could get a recording contract. Her English was good too. And then she said... She said..." Her gaze went blank, and he was suddenly reminded of Louise Jones.

Trying to keep his tone casual, he asked, "What did she say then?"

Margay shook her head and seemed to come out of it. "Who?"

"The Bard. What did the Bard say when you went back to her dressing room?"

She frowned at him as if he were crazy. "We didn't go back to her dressing room. We just listened from the audience."

"And there you go," Grant said, suspicions confirmed.

"What are you talking about?"

"You just pulled a Mrs. Jones. You were talking about going to that Bard's dressing room with Austin. You said she reminded you of Raven and you told her she should go to the States."

"No, I..." Her face twisted in a grimace, one hand going to her temple. "Christ, my head hurts."

Just like it did before, he thought. He was positive now that his suspicions were correct. "You're under a spell, Margay. And Austin is in this thing up to his neck. He took you to see that Bard. I'd bet a year's worth of paychecks they tried to recruit you to help with the bombing, and you told them to fuck off. Then the Bard made you forget that you'd even spoken to her. Just like she's probably been running around talking to those protesters today." He blew out a breath. "We have *got* to break that spell."

Margay shook her head, eyes squinted as if her migraine was back. "No, you're wrong. I talked to the ACIS investigators looking into the bombing, and they found no sign of magical influence."

"But they *did* think you could be under the influence of something?"

She rubbed her temples harder, eyes squeezed shut. "Yeah, they wondered about it, but there was no sign of anything."

"Or maybe there was, and they don't remember it either. I think we need to make a trip to Laurelton. If you're under a spell, Genevieve Briggs and her Arc friends would be able to break it. Then we get the whole lot of them *and* their Feral husbands out here to find Austin and his Bard girlfriend."

"That… might work, though I'm not sure there's anything there." Margay smiled, but it looked a little tight. "Which if you're right, may be a very good reason to assume there is."

"Come on, let's get dressed and get you some Tylenol and a couple more bottles of PowerUp while I make some calls."

* * *

"How's life in Mayberry?" Genevieve Briggs asked, a teasing note in her voice.

"Unfortunately, we've got problems a little more pressing than Otis the town drunk."

"Yeah, I saw the news. How's Margay?" Gen had

never actually met Margay, but she'd heard Grant talking about her plenty.

"Yeah, that's the problem. Is Kurt there? If he is, would you put this on speaker? I'd like his input."

"Then you're in luck, because so are Jake and Erica Nolan. We're helping Dave and Ariel work on their act -- they're getting ready to go on tour."

At that, Margay's eyes lit up. The PowerUp must be helping. "Dave? Dave Frost?"

"Margay's a fan," Grant said.

"Always happy to talk to a fan," Dave called. Like Margay, he'd melded with his Familiar. Unlike Margay, Dave had been killed in combat and trapped in the tiger's body. He used magic to talk -- and talking was Dave's best thing. The Feral was huge on YouTube, where two million subscribers checked in daily to enjoy his jokes, celebrity impressions, and acid sarcasm about everything from politics to culture.

Grant quickly described the situation, including Margay's account of what happened at the Familiar bunker, though without mentioning the country it was located in. The fact that nobody asked about those details revealed that everyone involved had filled in the blanks. He detailed her contradictory accounts of the Bard's involvement.

"That's not just a Bard," Genevieve said at last. "A Bard's magic would have worn off months ago. There's an Arcanist spell reinforcing it, maybe with the help of a potion or two. But there's definitely an Arcanist."

"The spell must be beginning to wear off, or she wouldn't even have remembered that much," Ariel said. "That's good news because it means the Arc hasn't been refreshing the spell. Give it a couple of weeks, and it'll be worn off completely."

"What about the protesters?" Margay asked. "How long are they going to be gunning for us, assuming this Bard's spells are what's causing the problem?"

"Depends on if there's an Arcanist reinforcing them," Erica said. "If it's just a Bard, it'll wear off by tomorrow. If it's a Bard and an Arcanist... Depends on how strong they are."

Everyone considered the implications of that for a long, uneasy moment.

"If you want," Genevieve said at last, "we could come to the restaurant and create a working on the sidewalk out front that would break any hostile spell present. That would keep the protesters who were under magical influence from picketing. They'd immediately come to their senses."

"Wouldn't do a damn thing for the actual Humanists, though, more's the pity," Dave pointed out.

"Actually, I'm more concerned about any possible spells on Margay," Grant said. "For that matter, we can't be sure I'm not under the influence too."

There was another thoughtful silence. "With all three of us Arcs working on it, we should be able to break just about anything cast by just about anybody," Genevieve said at last. "But I think it would be better if you both come here. We've got some permanent workings that would kill whatever nasties anyone's laid on you."

"I'd appreciate it," Margay said, "Also, there's the Austin problem. His cat weighed north of six hundred pounds, and in any straight up fight..."

"Yeah, well, he's not going to want to mess with me," Dave growled. "Any asshole who tried to blow up thirty Familiars and Ferals needs an appointment with my teeth."

"And mine," Kurt agreed.

"I'm in," Jake said. "I've been itching to teach those Russians a thing or two…"

"Who said anything about Russians?" Margay asked, a little archly.

"Oh, please," Dave said. "Everybody knows Ukraine is ass-deep in CIA. And since the Russians love to use magical agents to do their dirty work…"

"We'll take any and all the help we can get," Grant said, "Especially any that would help us even the odds."

"For that matter, we can see if the Feds would be interested," Erica pointed out.

"I actually tried that when this mess started," Grant said. "The Charlotte office turned me down. I got the impression they think this is probably a prank, since nobody actually died."

"Well, they've certainly been trying like hell to get someone killed. Particularly you two," Jake put in.

"Is there any way you can get over here tonight?" Genevieve asked. "This sounds pretty time sensitive to me."

Grant and Margay exchanged a look, and he said, "That's no problem."

"After we get the spells taken care of, I don't have any problem with closing BFS tomorrow and coming to Ashburg to give you a hand," Kurt said.

"We can all follow you back and start taking care of business," Dave said.

"My house isn't that big, but I can put y'all up if you don't mind close quarters," Grant said.

Then he hesitated, thinking it through. "I'm going to have to contact my second-in-command at the

Ashburg PD and tell him he's in charge until I get back. And I'd better call the mayor to let him know I'm leaving town for a consultation."

"Think he's going to be an asshole about it?" Dave asked.

Grant shrugged. "It's hard to tell with Miller. Besides, there's always the chance the Bard got to him too. On the other hand, he didn't show up at the protest today, so that's something."

"In the meantime, we'll start getting everything ready for you," Genevieve said.

"Sounds good. Margay and I will be there in about an hour." They said their goodbyes and hung up.

Next Grant called Roger Porter to let him know he was in charge while Grant was out of town.

"What are you up to, boss?" the older cop asked.

"Hopefully getting us some backup so these fucking Talents quit screwing with us."

Roger grunted in agreement. "I hear that. Watch your six."

The mayor was next.

Sean Miller didn't even say hello. "Hope this isn't about that mess with the Spoon again." His voice was noticeably chilly.

"Afraid so. I've got to leave Ashburg to do a consultation in Laurelton. I'll probably be gone a few hours. Roger Porter's going to hold down the fort for me while I'm out of town. I need to talk to some Talent experts I know about the situation." He decided mentioning spells was definitely a bad idea.

"Yeah, I want to talk to you about that too," Miller said, his voice going from chill to downright arctic. "My phone has been ringing off the hook with people raising hell about your kitty cat girlfriend. Why haven't you charged her with the Bright Act?"

"Because she didn't violate the Bright Act," Grant said patiently. "She thought they had a mass shooter, so she manifested. She didn't injure anybody - - she maintained control."

"But she did scare the living shit out of everybody there," Miller retorted. "And what's worse, people saw you leave her apartment yesterday and again today. One caller's threatening to inform the media about your conflict of interest."

Grant felt a hot flush of temper. "My personal life has nothing to do with this case."

"The hell it doesn't! What happens when the media starts asking questions about why the guy who's doing the cat lady hasn't arrested her yet for terrorizing the people of this town?"

"She didn't do anything to get arrested for!"

"I don't care. *Arrest her.* Let the courts decide whether she's guilty or not. Your job is to bust people who violate the law."

"Exactly. And she didn't. That's why I'm not making an arrest."

Miller's voice rose to a shout. "Goddamn it, *you work for me*! You'll do whatever the hell I tell you to do!"

"Like violating her rights? So that when she sues, the jury awards her millions Ashburg doesn't have?"

"I'm running for the South Carolina House, damn it," the mayor growled. "I don't want to look like a Talent hugger. Put that furry bitch in handcuffs and take her to a cell or you're fired."

"Sean, you know damn well you can't fire me without a town council vote." Grant had checked out Ashburg's laws concerning the chief's job before he'd even accepted the position. He probably knew them better than Miller did. *But then, the mayor's a fucking moron.*

"Then I'll call an emergency meeting. So get out of bed and put handcuffs on your girlfriend. She might even like it."

"No," Grant gritted through his teeth. "I'm not going to put a woman in jail to help your campaign."

"Then you are *fired*."

"Not without that vote, I'm not."

Sizzling silence fell for several long moments before Miller said, "I'm calling that meeting tonight. I suggest you show up with her booking photo or you're gone."

Chapter Eleven

"The mayor has cop's balls in vise," Karl Makarovich said, grinning in satisfaction. They'd bugged the Chief's home and office at the same time they'd bugged the Whitfields' apartment and the Spoon -- before they'd even put the plan into operation.

Now the three sat in their AirBnB's kitchen, listening to the bedroom bug via an app on Anastasia's cell phone.

"I told you telling Miller I was a reporter would work," she said smugly. The man had been more than happy to meet with her after the riot failed, either in hopes of damage control or in order to get his name on television.

They fell silent to listen as Margay and Grant argued.

"Look," the Feral was saying, "if you need to arrest me, I can make bail."

"Forget that," Grant snapped. "God knows what those assholes would do while you were locked up, waiting for a bail hearing. You could get out to find they'd burned the restaurant to the ground."

"That's not a bad idea," Austin growled.

Anastasia slanted him an amused look. Listening to Margay and Grant make love had driven the Feral into a jealous rage made all the more acute when his ex said Grant was a better lover.

So much for Austin's belief that Margay was still helplessly in love… Turned out, not so much.

All to the good. I can lead Austin around by his ego as well as his dick.

After a discussion, Margay and Grant decided to

change into something more appropriate to working spells. Since the Feral hadn't brought anything else to wear, they'd have to return to her apartment.

The team listened to the rustle of clothing as the couple dressed. Then the bug started picking up the familiar metallic sounds of a weapon being loaded.

"What's with the gun? You think they're going to ambush us on the way?" Margay asked. "How would they even know where we're going?"

"I don't put it past the Mayor to tell them. Especially if that Bard has been talking to him."

"That bitch is full of surprises."

"Why, thank you," Anastasia murmured, her smile sly.

"This Grant," Karl said, frowning. Karl always worried. "He is too smart for norm."

"He's a fucking canapé," Austin snapped. "I'd eat him in one bite."

Anastasia gave that the attention it deserved by ignoring it completely. "We need to take care of the chief and his woman *now*. I don't care to deal with his friends. They have a long history of fucking up the plans of very powerful people."

"Short notice to plan assassination," Karl pointed out.

"We don't have much choice. We can't let them get to Laurelton. Fighting all those Ferals -- including a flesh-and-blood tiger -- isn't anything I care to do." She fell silent, her mind working. "But I think I have an idea that should do the job."

Nodding decisively, she looked at the two men. "Start packing up while I make some calls. We're out of here."

* * *

"I don't know about this," Jimmy Miller said uneasily. "I mean, a lot of things can go wrong." The dead, eyes blind and staring. Bodies crushed and mangled, nothing but raw meat and spilled guts.

Now all those remembered corpses were wearing his face.

"But you want to be a hero, don't you, Jimmy?" Anastasia purred, her voice low and rich, as if God had boiled pure sex down into a syrup and poured it over her vocal cords.

Jimmy could listen to her talk for hours. He *had* listened to her for an hour just yesterday as she told him about all the evil Margay Whitfield had done overseas -- the way she'd battled Putin's benevolent efforts to free Ukraine from its corrupt Nazi government. Now that Whitfield was back in the States, she and her Satanist buddies were out to destroy the US government too. Not to mention the lives of norms like him.

"You want your family to be proud of you," Anastasia said. "That demon-possessed bitch is going to start killing people sooner or later. Meanwhile she's got Sawyer wrapped around her little Black finger."

"I know," he said, torn. Afraid, yet excited, adrenaline and arousal jittering through his body.

"You'll be a hero, Jimmy," she purred in that delicious voice. "You'll be *my* hero. Everybody will know what you did -- the risks you took. They'll know and they'll respect you just the way you've always wanted."

The thought of being Anastasia's hero made his heart pound. *She'll be real grateful when the bitch is dead.*

"When the time comes, you'll get one chance -- you can't hesitate. You've got to be my hero, Jimmy. Nobody else can do this. Nobody but you, Jimmy."

"I know. I won't fail you." He'd never been a coward, no matter what the family thought. This would let him prove to his father -- to all of them -- that he *wasn't* a fuckup. He was a man. A strong man. A brave man.

A *hero*.

* * *

Grant followed Margay across the apartment to the door to the stairs. She'd changed into running shoes, jeans, and a sweatshirt, appropriate to sitting on the ground in one of Genevieve Briggs's spell circles.

He was wearing jeans, boots and a sweater, along with a pancake holster with his backup pistol clipped to his belt. He carried the rifle bag over one shoulder. "Wish I'd had time to buy more bullets. Three mags won't be enough if your glow-in-the-dark ex shows up."

She paused to glower at him. "If you do run out of bullets, stay the hell away from him, Grant. I'll handle him. He would fucking eat you like a snickerdoodle."

Grant glowered right back. "You said his tiger is twice Raz's size. If you need help, I'm not gonna stand there and wring my fucking hands."

"No, because if he comes after us, I'm enclosing you in my manifestation. Where we'll both be safe."

Grant pictured Raz, frowning. She was a big cat, but he couldn't imagine there'd be that much room inside her. "Is she big enough?"

"A manifestation is whatever size we need it to be. Speaking of which…" She reached out to open the door to the street, and her manifestation burst golden around her in an explosion of sparks. "Wait here a minute. I want to make sure nobody's lying in wait."

Grant swung the weapons case off his shoulder and reached into it for the rifle. As he pulled the gun out, Raz flowed down the stairs, as silent as oil. The cat paused, listening, then Margay reached out of the manifestation and opened the door. Grant waited, ready to back her up, gun pointed at the ceiling, alert and ready as she slipped outside.

The tiger manifestation paused on the street, sniffing the air, Margay's breath clouding in the cold.

Grant stepped out onto the sidewalk, scanning the night cautiously while she locked up behind them. It was late, and Main Street was deserted of all but mannequins in store displays and flashing Christmas lights.

"Merry Christmas, motherfucker," Grant muttered, and used the key fob to unlock his Camry. It beeped cheerfully, and he opened the passenger door for Margay.

She banished the manifestation and got in. Grant safetied the weapon and handed it over, along with the rifle bag. "I want that in reach if we need it," he told her as he closed her door. "The back of my neck is itching."

As he slid in on the driver's side, she tucked the rifle back into the case and propped it in the floorboard between her feet. Her tiger rumbled, an uneasy note to her voice.

"Raz doesn't like this either," Margay murmured, her expression tense.

Grant looked both ways and pulled out, then did a K-turn. He had the green light, so he started across the intersection...

"Grant!" Margay screamed.

He slammed on brakes, the car fishtailing as he followed her gaze off to the right. Glimpsed moonlight flashing on chrome right outside her passenger window.

The crash thundered in his ears a heartbeat before something slapped him hard in the face. Margay shouted, her voice reverberating with her cat's panicked roar. The rifle bag in the floorboard flew up, slammed into her chin. Her shout cut off.

Grant desperately wrestled the bucking wheel as the Camry went into a spin. He heard a *crack* and a final *BOOM* as the car stopped with a second head-snapping impact.

A sudden, awful silence fell.

He sat dazed, his face aching. The smoky air smelled of gasoline, the sweet reek of antifreeze and burned oil. Beyond the cracked windshield, the hood of the car looked like a crushed beer can, and the vehicle sagged on one side, as if the right front wheel was bent beneath it.

What the hell did we hit?

"Margay?" He sounded slurred and drunk to his own ears. Stunned. "Margay, baby, are you okay?"

No answer.

His head swam as he turned toward her. Her seat sat at an angle to his, twisted half away from him toward the crumpled remains of the door. *The frame of the car is bent. Totaled it.*

The airbags had all deployed; they hung limply from the wheel, from the roof above the side windows, and the crumpled dash. Smoke lingered in the air, rank with the burnt rubber smell from the bags.

Margay's head hung as she sagged in her seat belt shoulder strap, her face curtained by her goddess braids.

Groaning, Grant fumbled with his seatbelt, managed to get it unlatched. Something wet ran down his face, probably blood from his burning nose and split lip. His shoulder ached savagely -- bruised all to hell from the belt's shoulder strap. He reached a shaking hand toward her. "Margay? Jesus, Margay, are you…?" His hand hit something lying half across her lap, half in the floor. He frowned at it. The rifle case?

Grant remembered a flash of an image: the bag flying through the air and slamming into Margay's head. Crap. He snaked a hand through her hair, searched over the slim, warm column of her throat until he found her pulse.

And blew out a breath in relief. *Oh, thank Jesus*! It still throbbed steadily against his fingers. Leaning in, he pulled her hair back to study her face and body, looking for blood. Sure enough, he glimpsed a snaking dark, wet trail down her chin. Probably from the rifle hitting her in the face. *Do I move her*?

Better not. If she had a brain injury or a broken neck, he could kill her. Leaning close, he explored her hanging head with gentle fingers. Looked like she was trapped between the seat and the crumpled door. Eying her position with the experience of a cop who'd worked way too many crashes, Grant felt his stomach sink. *It's going to take the Jaws of Life to get her out of this car.* "Margay? Raz?"

She didn't respond.

He looked around for what had hit them. A vehicle sat at an angle to theirs through what remained of the front windshield.

Holy shit, it's one of ours. The Ford Police Interceptor had rammed into the Camry's right front fender going damn fast. *Good thing I slammed on the brakes, or it would have hit Margay's driver's door dead on…*

And *killed* her.

He scanned the side of the Interceptor, spotted a number painted in blue. 10.

Jimmy Miller's unit. Fucking Jimmy Miller just tried to kill us. Because that was no accident. The SUV's headlights hadn't even been on.

But why the hell would Miller *do* something like that? The dumb bastard must have known ramming them was a good way to kill people, not least himself.

From the smashed front of the Ford, Grant had a sick feeling Miller had managed to do just that. *Need to check on the stupid prick. Where's my damn phone? Got to call 911…*

But even as he reached for the phone clip on his belt, he heard the scrape of footsteps on the pavement. When he glanced toward the sound, there was nothing there.

Oh shit.

"Cop still alive?" a voice asked in a guttural accent that reminded him of cold war movies from his childhood.

The Ford's driver's door creaked open, apparently under its own power.

A chill rolled over him as he realized whoever had opened the car door was wearing a Spook Suit.

"Nope, Miller's toast," a voice announced from empty air. Sounded like a New Yorker. "Looks like he took a chunk of debris through the head."

"Good," a female voice said, her tone dispassionate, as utterly without an accent as a network news anchor. "He fucked this up. He was supposed to T-bone the car, but he missed the passenger door by a mile."

"So what?" New York demanded. "Margay's out cold -- I can tell from her aura. I can just reach in and rip off her head." A feline rumble sounded.

Czar, Grant realized, feeling sick. *Austin. Has to be Austin the Ex. I fucking knew it.*

"What about Sawyer?" the woman asked.

Austin laughed, the sound snide and chilling. "That pussy is just a norm. Good for nothing but catching bullets. I'm going to enjoy dragging him out of that car when she comes around and twisting his head off while she watches." His voice raised to a mocking singsong. "'Oh, I love you, Grant. I never loved Austin.' Whore!"

You motherfucker. Moving slowly to avoid drawing attention, Grant lifted the rifle bag from Margay's lap. The zipper sighed as he opened it and reached inside to pull out the rifle. He dug the two spare magazines out of the bag and tucked them under one arm. "Margay?" Clicking off the safety, he chambered a round. "Margay, wake up, Austin and those fucking Talents are here."

"I'm going to enjoy this," Austin said.

Grant shot a hunted look out the front window toward the crunch and scrape of footsteps. Saw nothing. *I need to lure the bastards away from Margay. Give her a chance to wake up and join the fight.*

If she recovered consciousness. If she wasn't too badly hurt.

Scrrrrape.

He blew out a breath and shoved the Camry's door open, then popped to his feet to fire in the direction of the voices as he raced across the street. *BOOM! BOOM! BOOM!* "Norm *that*, motherfuckers!" he roared over the curses and startled shouts.

Good thing Main Street was dead this time of night. Or at least he hoped like hell it was.

Grant rounded the corner of the Mama's Spoon building, which was the last one on the row. He flattened his back against the wall as the Talents returned fire, weapons thundering, bullets whining past. When there was a pause -- reloading -- Grant dropped to one knee and started laying down a sweeping pattern of fire designed to hit anyone in the open.

Roaring in fury, Austin's manifestation ignited in a blazing gold glow. The tiger towered on its hind legs -- easy enough to do, given that it was only a magical field.

An image flashed through Grant's mind, sickening and vivid: the polar bear, dragging Deputy Steve Jenkins across Faraday Square as the Feral mauled him to death. The cop's helpless, horrified screams…

Not helpful, asshole, he told himself grimly.

Chips of brick hit his face as gunfire slapped into the wall. Grant lunged backward to his feet. Raised the rifle and ducked forward to shoot.

The gun clicked, empty. He jerked back as return fire slapped into the Spoon's building. Kneeling, he ejected the magazine, grabbed a fresh one from his back pocket, slotted it in and chambered a round. He pulled the cell off his belt, put it on the ground and dialed 911, then put it on speaker. Spotting a flash of muzzle fire from behind Miller's SUV, Grant brought up his rifle, aimed and fired. Someone yelped.

"911, what's your…"

"Ashford I-1," he spat. "I'm under…" *BOOM*! "…fire on Ashburg's Main Street…" *BOOM*! He ducked as a bullet whined past. "…Three suspects, armed with AR-15s. I've…" *BOOM*! "I've got my personal…" *BOOM*! "… Rifle. I need backup now. One of my officers has been killed after hitting my personal car in a patrol unit. My car's a Camry. I need SWAT and an ambulance now! My passenger is Margay Whitfield. She's injured and unconscious, trapped in my vehicle. Jaws of Life may be needed. One of my attackers is a Bard, and the other is a Feral who is fully manifested. I don't know what the third guy is. He sounds Russian."

There was an icy silence on the line. "Making false reports to 911 is illegal."

The line went dead.

Grant stared at the phone in sick disbelief for a moment. Then he realized what happened. *The fucking Bard got to 911.*

"Chief, we don't have to be enemies," a woman's voice called as the shooting stopped, her voice so richly seductive that for a moment he felt the pull. "Just come out and we can talk about it." Talking just a little too long, trying to bespell him.

For a moment he wavered. *Maybe she means it. Maybe if we talked it out...*

No. No, If I listen to that cunt, they'll kill Margay! He ground his teeth and forced himself to concentrate on getting a fix on the Bard's position. *I've got to save Margay. That's all that matters -- I can't let them kill her...*

"Come on, Chief! This doesn't have to end in blood..."

There. The voice was coming from across the street, right in front of the Tangled Web. He fired, fanning the weapon to lay down a sweep designed to get her even if she dodged.

He stopped firing. In the silence, he heard a choked sound, the scrape of something skidding on pavement. Maybe a shoe?

Then nothing.

Did I hit her? Given the Spook Suit, there was no way of telling. You could be dead or unconscious in one of those things and the only one who could find you was a magic user who could see the suit's glow.

"Anastasia?" the Russian called. "Anastasia?" A pause, before the man bellowed, fury and grief in his voice, "Fucker, I will rip off your head!"

"You're going to pay for that, asshole!" Austin roared, a terrifying note of rage in his voice. The massive tiger started toward him.

"Gotta catch me first, asshole," Grant muttered. He whirled and ran, pelting down the sidewalk. He knew this area better than these bastards did.

But how the hell am I going to hit these dickheads when they're invisible?

* * *

The sound of gunfire, Feral roaring, and furious shouts brought Margay to bleary, aching consciousness.

PAIN!

Something hard and viciously tight dug into her right leg, and her mouth tasted of blood. The reek of burned rubber filled her nose. Dazed, she looked around, trying to figure out where she was and what had happened.

For a moment she thought she was back in Ukraine. *Jesus, where're the recruits? Where's Austin?* "Austin?"

In the distance, she heard the thunder of Russian artillery fire and the answering Ukrainian *BOOOOOM*!

A flood of adrenaline shot her heart rate into a thundering gallop.

Rmmphhhh! Razia snarled low in her mind, shouldering into her consciousness. *RRRrrrroooooow*! The tiger gave her a furious mental push, and she snapped out of the flashback.

They were in a car -- or what was left of one -- not an armored personnel carrier. The right front of the vehicle was crumpled, the hood bent upward, blocking her view as it sat canted, as though one wheel was bent under it. The rags of a side-curtain airbag draped over her right shoulder. The seat beneath her was twisted sideways, and the door was partially crumpled inward. She twisted her head around, looking for the driver. There was no sign of anyone, and the driver's door hung open.

Beyond the shattered windshield, a figure of Santa stood in a store window display, his animated arm waving, a mindless grin on his face.

Grant. Where the fuck is Grant? The thought stabbed anxiety into her mind. She'd been in the car with Grant. They'd been on the way to Laurelton.

Where's Grant? He wouldn't have left me... The thought brought another blast of panic, echoed by the cracks of rifle fire.

She tried to move, only to freeze, gasping, as pain ripped through her right leg. Blinking muzzily, she realized the crumpled door trapped her right leg between it and the broken, twisted seat. When she tried to pull free, a blast of agony, raw and grinding, made her clench her teeth.

Oh, not good. She'd broken her leg once before during an MRAP rollover, and she recognized the pain. Her head throbbed like a cracked tooth, and reality skewed sideways again. *Where the hell am I? Is this Ukraine? Where's Austin?*

RRrrrraahhhhh! Raz said, doing something in her head. Everything made another twist and snapped back into place again.

Grant's car. I'm in Grant's car. Where is he? Raz, where's Grant? What happened to...

The familiar three-round *crack crack crack* of M4 fire echoed in the distance. No, not an M4, it was the civilian version, an AR-15. Grant was firing his weapon somewhere out there.

A tiger roared in answer, sending a cold spike of sheer terror through her.

Grant was firing at a tiger manifestation. Another spike of adrenaline crystallized her awareness, jerking her firmly into the present. *Austin. Austin's back. Austin's been behind all this shit. It was Austin at Grant's house. And now he's after Grant again.*

RRrrmmmmph, Raz agreed.

Shit shit shit shit shit. We've got to go save Grant. Even with an AR-15, Austin can kill him. One shot wasn't going to do it -- it took sustained fire to punch through a manifestation, and the bastard might kill Grant before he got off a long-enough burst.

RAWWWWWRR! The air around her vibrated with Raz's protective rage.

We have to manifest and pry my leg out of this mess, she told the cat.

Mmrrrrraaaooff. The spirit began to pour power into her, and she drew it in, spinning it into a tight, thin barrier around her trapped leg. Metal groaned as she began to expand the magical field…

* * *

Grant raced down the street alongside the building, then ducked behind it, his mind racing.

A thought flashed through his mind -- if the city council didn't fire him tonight, they would when they got a load of the property damage from the firefight. *I'll be lucky as hell to even be alive to have that problem.*

He listened to vile Russian curses as the two Talents ran toward his hiding place. He concentrated on remaining utterly still, keeping his breathing quiet, controlled, even as he prepared to throw himself out of the way if Austin realized he was there and attacked. An image flashed through his mind: a mouse dodging a cat, every move erratic. The idea of playing hapless prey to the traitorous piece of shit was enraging, but it was what it was.

A blaze of gold shot past as the tiger raced by. *Too damned pissed to pay attention to his cat's sense of smell.*

Grant didn't move, didn't even breathe. He focused on the running footsteps behind Austin.

One step. Two. The Russian had to be right in front of him. Now. He opened up, spraying bullets in a short, nasty arc.

Heard a strangled scream. Then nothing.

An ear-splitting roar rang out. Grant whirled and sprinted across the parking lot behind the Spoon. "You gutless little shit!" Austin bellowed.

Christ, he's right on my ass... Grant spun aside, and caught a flash of gold as the tiger's paw missed him by inches. He spun again, bringing the weapon up and shoving the muzzle right into the cat's open jaws. Austin recoiled, shouting, as Grant pulled the trigger -- *BANG BANG BANG!*

The Feral staggered, momentarily blinded by the gunfire right in his face. Grant didn't stop to see if it hurt him -- he just spun and ran again, weapon pointed at the sky.

Just up the block, he saw a car sitting under a streetlamp, three of its doors open. The bad guys'? He considered going after it... But Austin was right on his ass. In a straight-line run, Austin would catch him. And there was no guarantee the keys were in it anyway.

"Get back here, you fucking coward!" Austin

bellowed.

"Fuck off!" Grant muttered, and darted across the street to Campbell's Body Shop, heading for the gate of the ten-foot chain link fence. Pausing just long enough to aim, he put a round through the lock, jerked it open, and fled between the cars.

A shattering roar vibrated his chest, but he didn't look around as he raced behind a school bus. Crouching low, he hurried on, past an SUV, then something that had been an Acura before it lost a fight with an eighteen-wheeler on I-26. He'd worked that wreck.

He stopped in the shadow of a panel van. Looked like a bread truck.

"Guess you think you're pretty smart, don't you, normie?" Austin called. He sounded way too fucking close. "Just like that cunt of yours. You'll find out just how smart you are when I tear out your guts."

Grant froze, working to control his breathing. He'd emptied one magazine and he wasn't sure how many shots were left in the second. How the hell was he going to fight the Feral off if he ran out of bullets?

But every minute the bastard was chasing him through the junkyard gave Margay another minute to recover. Or at least, another minute help might come -- help that damn Bard hadn't managed to bespell.

Think, Grant. What can I make into a weapon? He scanned the darkness.

Too bad he had no way of knowing which of these cars were operational... Though God knew where the keys were.

Silence fell. No sound at all. It began to snow, flakes drifting downward. As he waited in the darkness, the chill cut through his sweater. Christ, it was cold. He heard the faintest crunch...

…Coming from overhead.

Sheer instinct had him leaping away from the truck, swinging his gun up. The tiger leaped from the top of the roof of the vehicle, and Grant sprang back -- not quite in time. A huge paw flashed out, raking a line of fire along his biceps. He bit back a scream and threw himself across the hood of a decrepit Saturn, narrowly avoiding the cat's next lunge.

"I like this game," Austin purred.

Grant pivoted and fired, backing away, pulling the trigger as fast as he could. Austin reared back, roaring, magic pouring off the cat as sparks and golden smoke. Falling snow hissed as it hit his magical field and instantly melted.

The gun clicked, empty. *Oh, shit.*

The tiger lunged at him and he twisted aside, groping for the last mag in his ass pocket. Spinning and ducking this way and that, trying to dodge as the cat chased him, sometimes rearing to strike out at him with glowing paws that smoked and sparked with magic.

Somehow Grant got the mag into the gun, chambered a round, and began to fire, blasting away as fast as he could right in the tiger's face. The manifestation leaped away, yowling. Countless dim lines cut across the manifestation's chest and head, magical scars from the raking paths of the bullets.

Then the gun clicked. Empty.

Austin laughed, the sound chilling. "You fucking moron. That one gun isn't going to save your ass. Because I don't think you've got any other mags, do you? I can just hunt you down and drag you back to Margay and let her watch me rip you apart."

The tiger stalked him, then threw himself into a lunge. Grant reversed the rifle and drove the butt into the mani's head. Czar roared and charged again, but Grant spun aside, his heart banging in his chest. He could feel a dozen cuts bleeding all up and down his body, though he hadn't been aware of the fucker actually hitting him.

He drew back the gun, meaning to swing it again…

Only to feel something grab hold of his rifle and jerk with a savage twist. The gun went flying. Grant spun, heart in his throat.

There was nothing there.

"Sorry, not so dead after all," said the empty air in a thick Russian accent.

An impact struck his head so savagely hard, he slammed into the side of a car with a thundering *bang*. Another blow hit, igniting double lights in his head, one from the fist in the face, one for his head hitting the car behind him.

"I'm going to beat you to death," the Russian snarled. To Austin, he added, "You can have whatever's left."

Grant threw up his arms, protecting his head, but another one of those blows hit him savagely right across the face.

As he staggered back, he could feel blood rolling down his face, one eye swelling shut. He reeled between two rusting hulks, keeping the big Russian between him and Austin. But since the fucker was also invisible, it was hard to tell if he succeeded.

How in the fuck do I hit something I can't see?

Then he spotted a thin plume of mist, rising up in the cold. He could just see it against the tiger's golden glow.

Which gave him an idea. But he was going to have to set this up, or the fuckers would realize what he was doing. He staggered as if he'd almost gone down.

"Pissing scared, norm?" Austin purred. "You should be. It's going to take us a long time to kill you."

"This fool waits for backup," the Russian said, with an ugly chuckle. "But Anastasia made calls."

Already figured that out, you prick.

"She told 911 to ignore any calls from you. As for the rest of the sheep, dispatch will tell them there's a live fire exercise at this end of the county," Austin said, circling Grant, who backed away. "Even your buddy Roger will ignore all the shooting. And the mayor's busy hiding under his desk from the demons."

From the corner of his eye, Grant watched that little plume of breath dance to the side. Saw the snow dusting broad shoulders.

He staggered again, falling back against a car. Watched the breath plume approach --

And ripped the gun out of the pancake holster still clipped to the back of his belt, threw himself to the side, and fired right in the center of the cloud's point of origin -- the Russian's mouth.

There was a bang as the invisible Russian fell back against the hood of a car, denting it in the shape of his body, then slid off the vehicle and hit the ground with a crunch.

Czar's big head swung as he watched the Russian fall. "Well, fuck," Austin drawled, then grinned at Grant. "Good shot. Saved me the trouble."

Grant slid to one side, trying to get room to get the hell away from the tiger. "You... don't sound upset."

Austin chuckled. "Those shitheads were planning to kill me anyway. Thought I didn't know. I'm a goddamn *tiger*. I could smell the lies on them, despite the Arc's spell charms. They're pretty good charms -- kept Margay from smelling my lies -- but I knew what to look for."

Czar reared, balancing weightlessly on his back legs, spreading huge forepaws. The tiger took a step toward him, its savage glow lighting up the junkyard around them.

"Well, ain't you lucky," Grant drawled in his best redneck Southern cop accent, even as he backed away, pointing the handgun up at the towering manifestation.

"I am, yes," Austin said in that smug, insufferable voice. "I can't believe you actually thought the cunt preferred *you* over *me*. Why in the hell would she love a useless norm? Can't see magic. Can't do shit."

"Well, considering I bagged two Talents today, I think I proved who is and is not useless."

"Yeah, well, your luck just ran out." He crouched, preparing to spring…

An explosion of gold rocketed out of the darkness and rammed into Austin's side like a cruise missile. "You treasonous son of a bitch!" Margay screamed, her voice edged in Razia's roar.

The impact knocked Czar ears over tail, and Margay leaped after him.

Grant stared in horror as the two big cats began to fight, ripping at each other with claws and teeth. Shit, Austin's tiger really was twice the size of Raz. Worse, it literally blazed in the darkness, far brighter than they were.

Austin's magic was every bit as strong as he'd bragged.

I've got to do something! He turned around, scanning the darkness frantically. He needed a

Goddamn weapon. Needed to get the furry fucker off Margay. Needed to *hurt* the bastard.

And then he remembered. *Yeah! Yeah, that might do it…If I'm lucky.*

He took off at a dead run, his head aching viciously with each stride, one eye swollen shut, a set of deep claw marks flinging blood as his arms pumped. He didn't even slow down.

No way in hell was he going to let that bastard have Margay.

He raced around the corner toward the only weapon he could think of, cursing his human slow body. Behind him, roars and hisses cut the night and magic sizzled and popped as the cats' warring magical fields ground against each other.

* * *

Margay dodged the swipe of a glowing paw and leaped, bounding ten feet in the air to land on Czar's back, the claws of all four paws digging into the manifestation's ribs. Raz's jaws clamped on to the back of the cat's neck where skull met spine.

An explosion of pain from warring magical fields lit up her senses, but she ignored it, biting harder, digging her claws in. *We held a Goddamn MEED. We can fucking rip off this bastard's head!*

Czar reared and slammed backward to land on top of her. Magic exploded in her senses, but she refused to let go, working her teeth and claws deeper and deeper into the manifestation.

"Let me go, whore!"

"Not on your life, traitor!" Margay told him even as Raz helped grind her glowing fangs into his magic. "You did this to us -- me and Raz and even Czar. You did it to your own cat, you betraying bastard!"

Czar flailed, roaring, and rolled with them, grinding right over her broken leg. The explosion of pain was so intense, so blinding, she lost her grip.

The tiger jerked away. Raz hissed as the huge beast twisted and pounced on them, claws tearing at her manifestation.

"I'm going to rip you apart, you little bitch! All this time, strutting around, pretending you were some big hero! Who did you blow to get those medals?"

She could feel her manifestation beginning to weaken. *I need to buy some time, reinforce my mani…*

Raz twisted, tore out of his grip and raced away, running right over a pair of cars, then bounding up and over the ten-foot chain-link fence to the street beyond. Margay bit back a scream as the landing slammed her weight into her broken leg. Even with Raz's manifestation supporting and protecting the shattered bone, it fucking hurt.

Even as she landed, she looked around to see Czar falling from the sky. She scrambled back, barely avoiding the tiger's pounce as she met Czar's mad, blazing eyes through the mask of her cat. "He betrayed you, Czar! *I* tried to save you. *I* did everything I could to save you, and he left you there to die. The worst Goddamn betrayal you can do to your own Familiar, Austin, you bastard! You betrayed your country. You betrayed me. You betrayed Czar!"

"*You had it coming*! None of you treated me as I deserved!" Austin shouted. "All you had to do was give me *what I deserved*. I wouldn't have thrown in with the fucking Russians. But nooooooo. The Corps was too busy being Woke! They gave it *all* to you just because you're Black and female and checked the right boxes -- and I *didn't*!"

As she backed away from him, she glimpsed

something rolling toward them. Coming up behind Austin. *Oh, yeah, baby!*

Got to keep Austin focused on me. The bastard always gets tunnel vision when he fights.

Knowing her cue, Raz began to roar at Czar in shattering bursts that blasted the air, Margay using her own magic to magnify the sound. Drowning out the sound of Grant's approach.

"Yeah, scream now, bitch! You just wait, I'm going to *really* make you scream!" Austin lunged toward her, but she danced away.

"You never made me scream!" she bellowed, magically projecting her voice until it was as loud as Raz's roar, drowning out every other sound as she led him into position. Staying just out of reach. "I was faking it every fucking time!"

Czar charged her, roaring, and Margay and Raz catapulted straight up like a housecat leaping away from a snake…

The Honda Prelude rammed into Austin's manifestation going sixty miles an hour. The tiger somersaulted over the hood, spun through the air, and slammed down behind it. The manifestation winked out, Austin screaming as he hit the ground.

"Did that hurt, motherfucker?" Margay spat, as she raced in the direction of the fallen Feral. "Good!" *Now. Now this ends!*

Except…

There was nothing there. *Shit, the bastard's still wearing his Spook Suit! How the hell am I going to keep him from getting away?*

"Czar!" Austin shouted, apparently not realizing he was invisible. "I need our mani! She's…"

A glowing hand appeared, reached upward.

Margay froze, prepared to fight.

"What are you doing?" Austin demanded. "Damn it, Czar…"

The hand reached up, grabbed something, pulled it away.

And Austin's face, stripped of its Spook Suit mask, blinked up into the falling snow, his expression confused. She had no idea why she'd never seen how weak his chin was. "What the hell?"

Margay grinned. "Why, thank you, Czar."

An expression of horror crossed the Feral's face. "Czar! We've got to manifest or we're finished!"

"I don't think he appreciates you killing him, Austin," Margay told him. "I think he wants me to return the favor."

"No!" Austin shouted.

Margay and Raz struck, glowing forepaw a blur of light as it slammed into Austin's head, claws extended. The crack of his neck breaking was very loud in the sudden silence.

Breathing hard, Margay stared down at the body. "Now you got what you deserved."

"He certainly did."

She looked around as Grant limped toward her, leaving the car sitting at an angle in the middle of the street. From what she could see from its front end, he'd totaled it. "Second car crash in one night," he said, wiping the blood off his lip. "And I'm getting royally sick of eating airbag."

"I'd imagine so. You okay?"

He shrugged. "Little dizzy."

She grimaced. "Yeah, I know how you feel. Where'd you get that car, anyway?"

Grant shrugged. "I think it belonged to the bad guys. They left it parked up the street with the keys in it. I saw it while I was running from this asshole. So while you argued with the shithead, I went back and got it. I figured that since it took a big impact to break a manifestation, a car might do the trick."

"Nice thinking outside the box." She sighed, exhausted, her head throbbing. She needed to drop the manifestation, but that leg...

"*Rmmmmmmmph,*" Razia said. The manifestation twisted, reformed around her into a glowing shell in the form of her own body. Helping support the broken leg.

"Hey, that's perfect," Margay said, pleased.

Grant lifted his brows. "She did that by herself?"

"Yep. We're blending a lot better."

"Speaking of blending..." He stepped up to her and encircled her with his arms, wincing only a little as the manifestation's magic nipped at his skin. He lowered his head...

The manifestation disappeared from around her head, and he kissed her, slow and deep. Despite her pain, despite her exhaustion, she opened to him, glorying in the slide and thrust of his tongue.

He drew back, staring into her eyes. She fell into his, into the love and admiration and need. "I love you," he said, his voice low. "I know I'm supposed to do this on the beach at sunrise with a ten-thousand-dollar ring and a camera crew... But fuck it." He took a deep breath, and she saw the need, the vulnerability in his eyes. "Margay Whitfield, will you marry me?"

"Yes!" The words were out of her mouth before she had a chance to think. Not that she needed to. She could feel the grin spread across her face, the sheer, giddy joy rolling over her despite the headache, the broken leg. "Who gives a damn about beaches and rings? You fought a *tiger* for me." She threw her arms around him, and he held her close as they kissed.

Until flashing blue lights made them draw apart to see the Ford Interceptor roll up. "Oh, hell, what now?" Margay muttered as they tensed.

The Ford's door opened and Roger got out, looking guilty and a little sick. "What the hell happened?"

Grant pulled Margay closer. "Talents happened."

Roger lifted a graying brow at Margay. "So I see. But I was referring to Miller and the wrecked cars, not to mention the bullet holes in Main Street businesses. It looks like you fought a war."

"We did." Margay eyed him right back. "Where the hell have you been, Roger? Grant had to take on those bastards by himself while I was pinned in the freaking wreckage."

Roger winced. "Damned if I know. I kept hearing all kinds of roaring and screams from this end of town, but every time I started to drive over here, I just… forgot where I was going. I was beginning to wonder if somebody had spiked my coffee." He shook his head. "I'm sorry as hell about that, Grant. If you want to fire me…"

"It wasn't your fault," Grant told him. "Austin gloated that the Bard called and bespelled you before they came after us. Did the same thing to 911 too, which is why they told me to fuck off when I called them in the middle of the firefight."

"Jesus." But he looked guiltily relieved. "I did get this weird call right after you hung up from telling me you were going to Laurelton. Some woman, though I can't quite remember what she said." He looked around. "Boy, this is going to be a fucking mess to explain."

Grant sighed. "Yeah. I'm going to have to call SLED. That investigation is going to be fun."

Margay frowned. Her giddy high was subsiding into a vicious backlash headache, and her leg was throbbing in time to her heartbeat, manifestation or no manifestation. Which was probably why it was so hard to understand why he had to call state law enforcement. "Why?"

"Because we've left at least four corpses all over town, one of them the mayor's nephew, the other three wearing Spook Suits. And that's aside from the property damage. If the town council hasn't fired me yet, they will when they see all the damage."

Roger eyed him. "You can call them all on the way to the ER. You're both bleeding from multiple wounds. Get in the car and I'll take you to the hospital."

"Not until I find the bodies," Margay told him. "Otherwise people are going to be running over them, since they're still wearing Spook Suits."

Epilogue

Six Months Later

The wedding cake towered on the table in the center of the Ashburg Baptist Church reception hall. It was a huge confection, its white icing adorned with skillfully piped *Piñata* climbing roses in shades of yellow and orange shading into pink, interspaced with equally exuberant tiger lilies.

On the cake's top tier, the bride and groom kissed, with a fondant Razia lying curved around them, looking smug.

The surrounding tables were loaded down with crystal bowls of fruit sculpted into flowers and trays piled with *hors d'oeuvres*. Jocelyn had outdone herself for her daughter's wedding, as everybody in town had known she would.

"Damn, this place is packed," Kurt Briggs said, staring around at the long room, which was decorated with live *Piñata* roses and tiger lilies, not to mention matching balloons and streamers of ribbon.

"They knew Margay's mom was going to be cooking," Dave Frost told him. The tiger was wearing one of his service animal vests, but rather than being his usual orange, it was dove gray with a white bow tie and a tiger lily boutonniere. It was his version of the dove-gray tux the groom and the rest of the groomsmen wore.

"Apparently all is forgiven," Roger said dryly to Grant, looking distinguished in his own gray tux.

"Well, not all," Grant murmured, sipping his champagne. Among the conspicuously absent were all the members of the Ashburg town council, which had indeed fired him.

Though at least they'd had the decency to issue Margay and Jocelyn a formal apology.

"When do you start work?" Genevieve Briggs asked.

He grinned. The Laurelton Police Department had offered him the chief's job after the prior occupant announced his retirement last month. "Two weeks from now. Basically, after we get back from our honeymoon." Suspecting he looked insufferably smug, he watched Margay circulate among the crowd. She looked breathtaking in an off-the-shoulder gown covered in white lace, her train and veil gathered over one arm, her lovely face alight, her bouquet of tiger lilies and *Piñata* roses in her free hand.

A flash went off as the wedding photographer snapped a shot of Margay laughing, her head tossed back in delight.

As he watched, Louise Jones tapped her on the shoulder, and Margay turned to greet their elderly teacher, then drew her into a hug.

Grant smiled, remembering his bride looking up at him through the lace of her veil, her golden eyes mysterious, her smile a seductive curve. *Mine*, he thought, in happy greed. *Mine mine mine…*

Which was something of a miracle. For a couple of months there, they'd been genuinely afraid their happily-ever-after was going to end in one of them going to jail.

Then SLED had released the video from Jimmy Miller's body cam, the Main Street store cameras and Joe's Body Shop. Joe, it seemed, had cameras all over his lot, which had caught most of the action. The footage had promptly gone viral, given Grant's connection to the Virgil Ford and President Roth cases.

In the end, the state had declined to prosecute

Grant and Margay for any of the mayhem, since it was obvious they'd been defending themselves.

The national consensus was that he and Margay were the victims in some mysterious Russian plot with the assistance of a traitorous Feral, though the connection to Ukraine had remained buried.

Even so, enough of the story emerged to turn them into national heroes. Margay and Grant had done a number of network interviews. They'd even talked to Darius Palmer of WSAG -- once he'd groveled.

To top it all off, *Magical Kitchens* had hired Jocelyn to judge the coming season of the show. Which was probably why Mayor Miller had reluctantly offered Jocelyn a full apology for some of the garbage he'd said after the Main Street shit tsunami.

Apparently, the town council was desperate to keep her from moving Mama's Spoon to New Orleans. Especially since the Spoon was already showing signs of being a hotter tourist attraction than ever.

Take that, Humanist Yelp trolls.

Ariel Frost stepped from the crowd to drop a hand on her husband's back. The lovely Arcanist wore one of the butter-yellow bridesmaid's gowns, its color making her red hair appear to glow.

"Hey, baby!" Dave looked up at her, flashing fangs in a way that would have alarmed anyone who didn't know him.

"Did you see all the live trucks parked on the hill?" she asked him. "The last time I saw so many cameras, we were shooting *Arcane Island.*"

Margay had become friends with Ariel, Erica and Genevieve during the nerve-racking period while SLED had been deciding whether to charge her and Grant. She'd ended up asking the three women to serve as her bridesmaids, along with Brenda Hollings, the Spoon's longtime waitress, and Nancy, who'd served as her Matron of Honor.

Jocelyn bustled out of the crowd looking lovely in a rose gold gown, if more than a little harried. "Gather around, everybody! Time to cut the cake!"

The crowd moved in, but made a path for Margay.

For a moment, her eyes met Grant's, and the smile that burst across her face like sunrise made his heart lift. She glided toward him, no sign of remaining stiffness in her leg.

She'd made a full recovery from her injuries. Her V.A. psychiatrist had given her a clean bill of mental health -- she and Raz had fully melded the night of that last battle. Even her PTSD nightmares had decreased, and her doctor thought they'd eventually fade completely.

Grant took her hand, and they smiled into each other's eyes, united in a sweet joy for a moment. Then they turned toward Nancy, who was carefully removing the top tier -- they'd eat that one on their first anniversary -- and transferring it into a small bakery box.

Jocelyn traded Margay the cake cutter for the bouquet. Smiling radiantly, her daughter let her train and veil slide from her arm. Nancy moved in to straighten the mass of lace and seed pearls for the photographer.

Grant stepped in close, inhaling the sweet spice of her perfume, tinged with that elusive scent he'd come to associate with her magic. He wrapped his fingers around Margay's as she held the cake cutter, loving the feeling of her smooth, warm hand.

They paused to let the photographer get into position, then carefully cut a piece from the bottom layer of the cake. But as they started to transfer it to a plate, it toppled off the cake cutter. Before it could hit the floor, a glowing paw shot out of Margay's skirt and caught it neatly out of the air.

"Yeah, baby!" Grant cheered. "Nice catch, Raz!"

The tiger rumbled, sounding smug. Margay scooped the piece off her magical paw, broke it in two, and handed half to Grant.

Their eyes met, and they stepped together. And Margay darted a hand in with the cake to leave a daub of icing on the end of his nose. She laughed, and Grant returned the favor, then popped the cake into her mouth. Margay caught his fingers between her lips and gave them a teasing lick.

They leaned in for the kiss at the same time, tasting butter cream and pineapple and magic as the guests burst into cheers and applause.

Which was when Dave launched into "Hakuna Matata," from the *Lion King*. The crowd laughed and began to sing along.

Margay whispered against Grant's mouth, "For the rest of our days, I'm going to love you."

"And I'll always be yours," he breathed back.

Raz strolled from Margay's skirts, paused to give everybody enough time to brace themselves, and roared.

Angela Knight

New York Times best-selling author Angela Knight has written and published more than sixty novels, novellas, and ebooks, including the Mageverse and Merlin's Legacy series. With a career spanning more than two decades, *Romantic Times Bookclub Magazine* has awarded her their Career Achievement award in Paranormal Romance, as well as two Reviewers' Choice awards for Best Erotic Romance and Best Werewolf Romance.

Angela is currently a writer, editor, and cover artist for Changeling Press LLC. She also teaches online writing courses. Besides her fiction work, Angela's writing career includes a decade as an award-winning South Carolina newspaper reporter. She lives in South Carolina with her husband, Michael, a thirty-year police veteran and detective with a local police department.

Angela at Changeling: changelingpress.com/ angela-knight-a-26

Changeling Press LLC

Contemporary Action Adventure, Sci-Fi, Steampunk, Dark Fantasy, Urban Fantasy, Paranormal, and BDSM Romance available in e-book, audio, and print format at ChangelingPress.com – MC Romance, Werewolves, Vampires, Dragons, Shapeshifters and Horror -- Tales from the edge of your imagination.

Where can I get Changeling Press Books?

Changeling Press e-books are available at ChangelingPress.com, Amazon, Apple Books, Barnes & Noble, Kobo, Smashwords, and other online retailers, including Everand Subscription and Kobo Subscription Services. Print books are available at Amazon, Barnes and Noble, and by ISBN special order through your local bookstores.

Changeling Press, LLC

ChangelingPress.com

www.ingramcontent.com/pod-product-compliance
Lightning Source LLC
Chambersburg PA
CBHW071151260626
47162CB00003B/998